Escape

Rye James

Maverick Spur Publishing

Escape

ISBN: 978-0-6151-7574-4

1

After a long 14 hour day at the office crunching numbers, Ray Spencer was looking forward to just having a late night dinner, and relax while watching an old movie. The stress of pouring through the books of the last five years for Hartwell Enterprises was beginning to take its toll on him. He began looking through the previous years books a couple weeks prior to that when he noticed a few errors that weren't corrected. He began working through the nights so he could work more freely, without having to worry about anyone looking over his shoulder. As a general rule all the accountants in the building were allowed to work as late as they wanted as long as they locked everything up when they were finished.

Spencer always made sure he had some work to do so no one would question why he stayed later. Just enough to finish after everyone left but not so much that it'd take up too much time away from looking through the books. It was the only way he could investigate the numbers without drawing attention to himself.

As he backtracked, he noticed several more errors. The company had misstated its numbers by millions of dollars to make the financial statements look good. The only person he confided in about this was his girlfriend Stacy. He wanted to wait until he completed looking through all the books before brought his findings to the company's supervisors.

Spencer was a very moralistic type of person. He was the kind of guy who believed in honesty and fair play. Loyal to his friends and family, he always tried to treat other people with respect. As an accountant he believed in the ethics code he'd taken to always report numbers accurately, whether they were good or bad.

Everybody else in the office had already left hours before when he finally decided to go home for the night. He put some papers in his briefcase that documented some of the accounting errors the company made before putting on his coat. He walked out of his office, and looked around to make sure nobody had returned to the building. As he walked through the hallways he periodically stopped to look behind him, not being able to shake the feeling he was being followed. He kept shrugging it off to his paranoia though.

He decided to walk down the stairs instead of using the elevator. Maybe he'd seen too many movies but he was wary of using an elevator and not knowing what'd be there when it opened. He walked down several flights of stairs till he got to the ground floor without any problems.

Once he finally left the building, he sprinted to his car, trying to avoid as much of the heavy rain as possible. Quickly unlocking his door, he just sat in his black Acura watching the falling rain. He wondered if he was doing the right thing sneaking around looking through the books. He wasn't even sure what he was trying to find, and he knew they'd eventually find out what he was doing. He thought maybe he should just stop looking for errors and worry about his own job.

He started his car, and was about to clear the rain from the windshield, when he noticed a piece of paper stuck to the wipers. Spencer at first thought that maybe the wind had blown it onto his car, but upon looking more closely, realized it had been put there. It had been folded, and was firmly entrenched between the wiper and the windshield. He opened his door and reached his arm around to the windshield, and pulled the paper out from the wiper, and quickly got back in his car. He hoped the rain hadn't washed away any of the writing on it. He curiously unfolded the paper, and looked at both sides of it to make sure he wasn't missing anything. It simply said "WATCH OUT".

"Watch out. Watch out for what? For who?" He asked himself.

Spencer sat there a few minutes longer trying to think of who could've written the note. As short as the note was, he didn't notice any of the letters matching up to anyone's handwriting that he knew. He started to head for home where maybe he would be able to think more clearly. Driving through the streets, he popped in his favorite Billy Joel CD, which always seemed to relax him a little.

He reached his house in about half an hour. Spencer loved living in the suburbs. It was such a quiet neighborhood, which he envied after growing up in the hustle of the city. There was never any excess noise, or trouble in the area. Spencer passed by a blue car on the curb of his house before pulling into the driveway. He'd never seen the car before but he assumed it was someone visiting one of the neighbors. He got out of his car, and ran towards the door, with his briefcase covering his head from the rain.

The one thing he always hated about coming home though was not having someone greet him at the door. He missed not having a dog run up to him as he walked in, wagging it's tail, just wanting to be petted and play around. He figured it'd also be good to have a watchdog around, not that it was necessary, but just in case. But having a dog would mean changing his girlfriend's mind about the subject, which would be an almost impossible task. She wasn't much of a dog person, so he always relented about buying one.

He took off his coat and started shuffling through his mail when the phone started ringing. He hated hearing that as soon as he walked in the door. He assumed it'd be Stacy, since she usually called about 10 o'clock every night. He was caught off guard when he heard a man's voice at the other end of the line.

"Did you get my note?" The strange voice asked.

Spencer tried to recognize the voice, but it wasn't familiar to him.

"Watch out for what?"

"You're creating problems for yourself, Ray."

"What kind of problems?"

"Problems from people that you're not prepared to handle."

He was getting an eerie feeling listening to what the man was saying, but he couldn't just ignore what he was saying either.

"So what exactly are you trying to tell me?" Spencer asked.

"To watch yourself. Watch your back. And above all, don't trust anyone. The wheels have already been set in motion. They're coming for you."

"Who?"

"You'll find out soon enough."

"So how do I know I can trust you?"

"If you couldn't, you wouldn't be getting this phone call."

"Who are you?"

"Just a friend. That's it for now. I'll be in touch later. Remember to stay alert at all times. The moment you let your guard down you'll be dead."

Spencer just stared at the wall with the phone still pressed to his ear, listening to the buzz. The last thing the man said to him replayed in his head a few times over, not really sinking in that it could be true. He put the phone down, and took a gulp, wondering what he had gotten himself into. He hastily turned around, looking the room over for anything that might have seemed out of place. Everything appeared to be normal though. He then snapped his head up towards the window, remembering the blue car parked outside the house.

He slowly walked towards the window, and opened the curtains ever so slightly. He peered out the slit in the curtains looking at the car parked in front of the house. His mind started racing with thoughts of whose it could be. His mouth was dry, and he could feel his heart thumping heavily, like it was going to explode out of his chest any minute. He'd never felt such a presence of danger and uncertainty before.

Spencer loved the peace and quiet that the house usually afforded him, but now he wished there was a party that would've matched the hottest nightclub in Philadelphia. The uneasiness of being by himself at that moment, or hoping that he was alone, tied his throat up in knots and made his hands sweat. One thing he knew was that he wasn't going to be able to relax until he knew he was the only person in the house. He was going to have to search the house to put his mind at ease.

Spencer certainly wasn't about to go searching the house without some protection, so he walked into the kitchen and pulled a knife out of one of the drawers. There were two small rooms and a bathroom on both floors of the house. The two rooms on the first floor were his home office, and a game room. The two upstairs rooms were his bedroom and a guest room.

Gripping the knife in his right hand he gingerly walked into the bathroom. He put his free hand on the side of the shower curtain and strongly threw it to the side, ready to pounce on the intruder. To his relief, the shower was empty. He breathed a little easier for a few seconds. After he took a moment to settle down, it was time to search the other rooms.

He slowly opened the door to his office and flicked on the light. He quickly spun around behind the door as if someone was waiting there for him, but again, he was relieved to find nothing. There were few places where a person could hide in the downstairs rooms. Next up was his game room. He wiped the sweat across his forehead with his sleeve just before he entered the room. His head peeked around the door to once again find empty space. Although he was scared out of his mind at what he might find, it was a rush like he'd never experienced before.

Then Spencer thought he heard a noise coming from one of the upstairs rooms. It sounded to him like the floor creaking, like it does when someone's moving around. He tried to remain as calm as he possibly could, realizing that houses do creak a lot, and that it could be his paranoia playing around with his shot nerves. By this time, the knife in his hand had almost become glued to his palm with a deathlike grip.

He walked to the bottom of the stairs, and looked up towards the top, almost as if he was waiting for a push from someone to proceed. He took a deep sigh and started to walk up the stairs. He took to each step slowly and methodically, carefully trying to avoid making any sounds. When he reached the top of the stairs, he went straight ahead into the bathroom. He was glad this one had a clear shower door that he could see through from a distance. He hoped that this wouldn't be a nightly occurrence, as he didn't think he'd be able to handle it.

As he walked into the guest room, he heard a slight rattle to the left of him. Spencer instantly looked over, with his eyes bulging out, only to discover it was the shaking of the window from wind of the storm. Breathing rather heavily, he quickly flicked up the light switch on the wall, and looked to the right to see an empty closet. He then saw the bed, which was directly against the far wall. Walking towards it, he thought hiding under the bed was something that was only done in movies, but he had to check. He slipped down to his knees and lifted up the sheets of the bed, not finding anything.

He stood back up, breathing heavily once again, knowing there was only one more room to go. Although relieved to not have found any surprises thus far, Spencer knew that his bedroom would be the most likely spot for someone to be waiting for him. Maybe that's why he saved it for last, procrastinating looking in that room, though he knew he had to. He stood at the door and closed his eyes, like he was praying for everything to be alright. When he opened his eyes he felt a slight chill come across him, and felt goosebumps popping up on his arms.

Gently turning the knob of the door, Spencer opened it just enough to be able to turn on the light. He flipped the switch up, but the room stayed dark. He quickly flipped it back down and up again, waiting for a different result.

"Oh, no", he thought.

He wished he could just turn back and pretend that he already looked in it and found nothing. Even if he did find nothing, he wondered how he'd be able to stay there if he was constantly looking over his shoulder. He opened the door a bit farther, and upon turning around the corner of the door saw the outline of a man dressed in black. The man was wearing all black from head to foot, including a mask over his head that only had an opening across his eyes and bridge of his nose.

Spencer's eyes first noticed the man's gun and placed his hand on the stranger's wrist. The sudden impact of Spencer's hand forced the man to pull the trigger of the gun with the bullet going into the floor. The gun had a silencer on it though, so no shots would be heard by anybody in the area. They wrestled with each other, neither man gaining an upper hand, before the momentum of the struggle carried them across the bed. While both men were trying to use their strength to gain an advantage, another shot fired, this time lodging into the corner of the ceiling.

After briefly feeling the warmth of the recently fired gun's barrel pressed against the side of his head, Spencer was able to muster up the strength of a bull before the trigger could be pulled, throwing the man off the bed. Spencer took a lamp off the table next to the bed, ripping the cord out of the wall, and threw it at the man before he had a chance to regain his composure and fire. As the man got back to his feet after ducking the lamp, Spencer then rushed towards him, kicking the gun from his hands. Spencer reached down onto the bed for the knife, but as he picked it up was met with strong resistance.

The stranger gained an advantage with his strength and forced Spencer up against the wall as they battled for control of the knife. The confrontation carried out into the short hallway at the top of the stairs. Spencer's foot slipped on the top step while grappling with the stranger, and both men began tumbling down the narrow staircase while still holding on to each other. They both hit the floor very hard, with Spencer hitting the back of his head on the wall.

Spencer was the first to get up, and noticed the black shirt of the man had turned to red on his right side. He then noticed the knife on the floor had a trickle of blood on it. The knife must've pierced his side falling down the stairs. Judging from the amount of blood on the knife, it didn't appear to be a deep wound. The stranger then began slightly moving around. It gave Spencer enough time to distance himself though as he ran out the front door into the pouring rain.

Spencer headed straight for his car and quickly padded down his shirt and pant pockets before realizing that he left his keys inside.

"Shit," he groaned.

He looked back at the house and noticed the man emerging from the doorway, and took off running down the street. He looked back a few times as he was running to see if he was being chased but didn't notice the man following. He cut through the lawn of one house and hopped a chain link fence, settling in behind a garbage can to catch his breath. His eyes were scanning all around for a glimpse of his pursuer, but saw no sign of him.

Now he had to think about where he was going. There was no way he could go back to his house anytime soon and risk being ambushed again. He reached into his back pocket making sure he still had his wallet, which he did. He opened it up and counted a hundred dollars, enough to get him a room at a hotel for the night. The Sports Haven, a local sports bar, wasn't too far away. If he could make that, he could clean himself up a little, and figure out what to do next.

After catching his breath, and not seeing any movement anywhere, Spencer decided it was time to move. He cut through the sides and back-yards of houses over the next few streets, trying to stay away from open spaces. As he reached the curb of one of the streets he heard the screech-ing sound of burning rubber. He aptly looked to the end of the street and to his horror saw that same blue car racing towards him with the head-lights blazing.

Spencer promptly cut across the street as the car sped at him. He hopped a few low fences and took cover behind a shed. He looked to the immediate area around him, checking for anything that he could use as a weapon. He didn't find anything though that would suit him. A few seconds later, he noticed the outline of a man a few houses down. It had to be his attacker. The man appeared to be looking for something, as he kept turning his head, looking out into the distance.

Although Spencer could tell the man wasn't wearing a hood any-more, he wasn't able to actually see his face. After a few more minutes of searching, though he didn't seem to be looking very hard, the man went back to his car. Spencer heard the shutting of the car door and saw the car drive past him. He couldn't be sure whether he was actually leaving though, or if he was just driving around looking for him.

Spencer squinted his eyes looking up to the sky, hoping the rain wouldn't let up. He was sure that the worse the weather was, the better his chances were of not being seen. Although he was drenched he didn't feel cold, in fact he hardly even noticed the rain pounding on him. He wiped the water from his eyes then started moving again. He went from house to house moving across the street in a zig zag pattern to be tougher to spot, stopping behind houses or objects that would conceal him.

It'd been about ten minutes since he'd seen that ominous looking blue car. Maybe the man, figuring the weather made it too difficult to find anybody, decided to stop searching for him tonight. But maybe he didn't really need to look for him. Maybe he would be waiting for him some-place like he was tonight.

Spencer had finally run out of streets to cross in the section. There was no place else to hide, and he couldn't stay out in the rain all night. He'd have to chance coming out into the open. He slowly came out from behind a house, carefully looking all around him. There were no signs of anything out of the ordinary.

As he walked down the road, Spencer suddenly noticed something moving. His eyes were aghast at what he saw. It was the outline of a man walking towards him. He briefly clenched his hands as the two men came closer. Before, he hardly even noticed the rain. But now, he couldn't tell if his hands and forehead were sweating, or if it was the rain that moistened his skin. He thought that even if it wasn't raining, he'd probably be just as drenched with perspiration as he was with the rain.

The two men were within twenty feet of each other, and Spencer was ready for anything. He starting thinking it had to be the man chasing him. Who else would be out walking in that kind of weather? Of course, maybe like himself, this guy had no choice either. He was starting to doubt his thoughts. Spencer kept his head down while keeping the man in his sights out of the corners of his eyes. He curled his hand up in a fist and was ready to pounce on the guy as he walked by.

"Some weather we're having huh?" the stranger said as he walked by.

"Yeah," Spencer replied.

Spencer immediately looked behind him and saw the man continuing his path. He felt a moment of relief as he continued walking. It'd only be a few more minutes before he got to the bar. He then thought about Stacy. She usually would leave a message for him when he got home before they talked. Chills suddenly overtook him as he began wondering if something had happened to her. The first thing he'd do when he got to the bar would be to call her and make sure she was OK.

By the time Spencer reached the bar, he couldn't shake the feeling that something had happened to Stacy. With the weather being as it was, it didn't appear to be too busy of a night for them. Still, there were quite a few cars in the parking lot. Spencer clung to the stones of the building, staring into the parking lot. He was looking for that blue car. He wasn't going to take a chance of being surprised again.

Though he saw a couple blue cars in the parking lot, they were not the same one that hounded Spencer. As soon as he entered the bar he noticed he was given a few looks, probably for being as wet as he was. He looked like he had just been swimming with his clothes on for a few hours. Spencer immediately went to the payphone and dialed Stacy's number. With every ring that wasn't answered he got even more worried. Finally, the phone was picked up.

"Hello?"

"Stacy."

"Ray? Ray, are you OK? I've been trying to call you at home, on your cell phone, where have you been?"

"Listen, I can't go home right now. Some stuff's happened, I'll tell you about it later, but right now I want you to get out of there."

"Why, what's wrong?"

"Just get what you need, and get out of there. There's no time to explain now."

"OK. Where are you at, I'll come pick you up?"

Spencer hesitated on telling her where he was. He could still hear the man on the phone saying, "don't trust anyone."

"Ray, you there?"

"Yeah, I'm here."

"Where are you?"

"The convenience store across from The Sports Haven bar. You know where I'm talking about?"

"Yeah, I'll be there in twenty minutes."

"OK. I'll be inside waiting for you."

After hanging up, Spencer couldn't stand the fact he was having doubts about his own girlfriend. He thought about it a little while longer when suddenly something she said struck him as being weird. How did she know he needed to be picked up? Or did she just say that assuming he didn't have a car? But why would she assume that? He hated the feeling that he couldn't trust anyone.

Spencer then went into the bathroom to try and clean himself up a little. He was leaning over the sink when he heard the door swing open, and saw a man walking in. His head snapped to attention watching the man.

"How you doin', man?" the patron asked.

"Good."

Spencer cautiously watched in the mirror as the man walked behind him. He didn't take his eyes off the man as he walked into one of the stalls behind him. He nervously turned around and looked at the floor underneath the stall the man went into. He didn't think it was the man who was after him, but he thought it'd be best to go out into the bar where there was a bunch of people around. He looked at the bar, and thinking he could really use a drink to settle his nerves, ordered himself a shot of bourbon.

"Looks like you've been in the rain a while," the bartender said.

"Yeah, car broke down. Had a little ways to walk. No big deal though."

He finished his drink, then Spencer left the bar, waiting for his girlfriend to show up. He watched the convenience store from the side of the bar, kneeling down in front of a car. The roof overhung a little so he wouldn't get wet, and he couldn't be spotted from a distance. The drink didn't settle his nerves as much as he hoped it would. He anxiously awaited Stacy showing up hoping the bad feeling he had about her would go away.

2

A half hour went by and there was still no sign of Stacy. Spencer began worrying that something happened to her. What seemed like a million thoughts crossed through his mind. Did the man who was after him go after her too? Was she just slowed down by the weather? He was just about to go back inside the bar and call her when he noticed a car park by the convenience store.

He was horrified to see that it was that menacing blue car that his attacker drove. He wondered what would happen if Stacy pulled in while he was there. Did he know what she looked like too? Spencer couldn't believe the timing of when the man showed up. Was he out looking for him all that time and finally gave up?

Spencer thought of how big a coincidence it was that the man showed up at the place he was to meet Stacy right after he called her. He started thinking of the phone call again and what he said about not trusting anyone. Was he talking about Stacy? He shook his head, like he was trying to rid himself of his thoughts. He refused to believe that Stacy had anything to do with it.

After sitting in his car for a few minutes, the stranger got out and walked into the store. Spencer still couldn't really get a good look at him though since he was still a pretty good distance away. About a minute later, the man came walking back out of the store and opened his car door to get back in, but suddenly stopped. He stood motionless for a second then turned his head towards the bar. He took a good hard look in that direction. Spencer's heart almost stopped thinking that the man knew he was over there.

A short minute later the blue car pulled into The Sports Haven parking lot. The stranger then parked his car and walked into the bar. Spencer kept himself down behind a car, hidden from the sight of his pursuer. A few minutes later, though it seemed like an eternity to Spencer, the man came walking back out and sat back in his car. Spencer watched him pull away and drive down the road out of view. There was no question in his mind that he was definitely looking for him. It didn't seem like he was just randomly picking spots either. He knew exactly where to look. Spencer's mind turned to Stacy again thinking she was mixed up in it.

Spencer spent the next few minutes trying to gather his thoughts and figure out what he was going to do next. He determined the first thing he'd do was go to Stacy's apartment to see if she was there. He had to find out if she was somehow mixed up in everything. After that, he'd call the police and let them know what was happening. Spencer heard a car door slam shut and looked over to find a cab dropping somebody off. He rushed over to it to see if it was available. He hopped into the back seat, happy to finally be out of the rain.

"Where to, man?" the cabbie asked.

"Midtown Apartment Complex."

"Be there in a jiffy."

Along the way, Spencer just stared out the window watching the rain. He started reflecting on his night and couldn't believe what was happening to him. If Stacy was involved, would his attacker be waiting for him at her apartment, thinking that he might show up there? It was a gamble he had to take though, if only for his own peace of mind.

"These things only happen in movies," he mumbled to himself.

What started out as just another day had turned into a nightmare that he never could've even dreamed about. By the time they got to the apartment complex the rain had lightened up quite a bit. It was just a steady drizzle now. Spencer let the cab driver know to stop a few apartments short of where he needed to be. Just in case the apartment was being watched, he might be able to sneak into it without being seen. He told the driver he'd be back in a few minutes and to wait for him.

The apartment complex was rows of apartments lined up horizontally to each other. There were sixteen apartments to a row with eight on the ground, and one above each one. They were small apartments, with most having a living area along with a kitchen, bathroom, and a bedroom. There was nothing fancy about them as mostly lower middle-class people lived in them.

Spencer walked around to Stacy's apartment and noticed that the lights were on. There were two entrances on the ground apartments, the front door or the porch to the back of it. He figured if someone was watching the apartment, they'd be looking for him to enter by the porch, so he decided to go in the front door. His heart was racing again, not knowing what to expect when he went inside.

Gently turning the knob, Spencer was a little surprised to find that the door was unlocked. He walked through the living room being very alert to even the slightest noise. He briefly glanced in the kitchen with no sign of Stacy. He walked back through the living room to get to the bedroom and noticed that the door to her room was slightly open. He put his eye to the crack in the door to see if he noticed anything unusual.

Spencer slowly pushed the door open and looked around the dark room. His eyes looked to the floor and noticed a leg sticking out from the other side of the bed. Spencer's chest felt like a hammer was pounding away on it as he approached the fallen body. He knelt down and turned the body over, looking at Stacy's lifeless face. She had been stabbed with a knife in her right side. He took her face in his hands and gently kissed her lips for the final time as tears started to run down his face.

A range of emotions passed through Spencer in a few short moments. His sadness quickly turned into bitterness and anger. He went into the living room to call the police, but noticed the line had been cut as he picked up the phone. He then remembered that she usually left her cell phone on the kitchen table when she was home. Upon entering the kitchen, Spencer noticed a piece of paper was underneath the phone.

Spencer picked up the phone with one hand and the paper with the other. The paper said "I'm Right Behind You." He nervously looked out of the corner of his eye expecting someone to pop up behind him. He took a gulp out of fear that he'd been trapped. Spencer spun around, getting ready for a fight, but was glad to see he was alone. He glanced around the room and looked to the porch to find that he was indeed by himself. The note must've meant in a figurative manner of speaking.

He thought about the paper he just found then recalled the one he found on his windshield earlier. Could they have both been written by the same person? The writing seemed different, but it was strange that two different people would have left notes like that, both short in the amount of words they used. He wondered if the man who called him on the phone was in actuality the same person who was waiting for him inside his room. If it were the same person, why would he warn him though? Spencer was having trouble figuring it all out.

Spencer's thoughts were broken by the unexpected ringing of the cell phone in his hand. He looked at it like the ring was tantalizing him. Although it was Stacy's phone, what if the killer knew he was there? After a few rings he decided to answer it.

"Hello?" Spencer cautiously answered.

"Ray, get out of there."

"Who's this?"

"It's a friend."

Spencer recognized the voice as the same one who called him earlier.

"How do I know you're not the guy who attacked me?"

"You've gotta trust me. And you've gotta trust me when I tell you to get out of there now."

"You told me not to trust anyone."

"That's right. Trust what you feel is right."

"My girlfriend's dead."

"I know."

"How do you know this number?"

"I know everything about you, Ray. But then again, so does he."

"Who is he?"

"It doesn't matter right now. First you have to get out of there. Go home and get anything you might need, cell phone, money, anything. Then go to a hotel for the night."

"You expect me to go back home?"

"Don't worry, he won't be there."

"How do you know?"

"Cause I know what he's thinking."

"What's that?"

"Just don't call the police. Now get out of there. I'll call later."

Spencer dropped the phone on the floor and rushed out of the apartment. He got in the cab and asked to be taken to his house. On the way there, he kept seeing Stacy's face appear in his mind. He sniffled and fought to hold back the tears. She didn't deserve what happened to her. If they wanted him, they should've left everybody else alone and just come after him alone. He didn't see what killing her accomplished when she wasn't involved in anything.

As Spencer exited the cab when it pulled in front of his house, he looked around for that blue car, or anything that didn't seem right. Everything was quiet just like it was any other night, like nothing had happened. He watched the cab drive down the road, then turned around and looked at his house wondering if there were any more surprises in store for him. He slowly and cautiously opened the door before going inside. It was almost becoming second nature to him. Every time he sees a door now, he'll wonder what's on the other side of it.

Spencer looked down at the small amount of blood on the floor along with the knife still lying there and wished he could close his eyes and make it all go away. He listened for any noises and quickly scanned the room for any intruders. With it seemingly clear, Spencer went into a drawer in one of the living room tables and pulled out some money that he kept there. The extra couple hundred dollars was enough to keep him going for at least the next few days. He remembered the papers he brought home from the office, and went to the table where he left his briefcase, but it was gone. His attacker must've taken it with him. He then picked up his cell phone and car keys off the table. He stopped and thought to see if there was anything else he needed, but in his stressed state of mind, that was all he could think of. A few moments later he bolted out the door.

Spencer started driving though he really wasn't sure where he was going. Anywhere would be better than where he's been. He stopped at a red light, and briefly glanced in the rear view mirror, before jerking his head back up to look more closely. Two cars behind him was a blue car that looked to be similar to the one that seemed to always be around. He felt like giving up if this was how it was going to be all the time. A resignation set inside of him that he was fighting a losing battle.

When the light turned green Spencer made a left turn to see if the car would follow him. Looking in his mirror he was disappointed to see the car turn immediately after him. Spencer maintained his speed, as did the car following him. It didn't seem to be in any hurry to catch up to him. Coming up to another corner, Spencer sped up a little and made a right hand turn. He noticed that the car behind him though didn't seem to increase its speed at all. He looked back up into the mirror in time to see the blue car continue driving straight ahead.

It must not have been the same car, he thought. Either that, or whoever it is, is in no hurry to finish off the job. He also thought maybe it wasn't a good idea to be driving his car. The man on his trail seemed to know everything about him and would be able to spot it a mile away. He came across an elementary school and figured it was as good a place as any to ditch the car.

Spencer parked the car on the grass and started walking. There was a hotel about twenty minutes away from there. He needed to lie down and rest for a little while. The events of the night had really shattered his nerves. He finally reached the hotel and checked in under the name Bob Smith. Not very original, but he didn't think it had to be as long as the name wasn't Ray Spencer.

Spencer unlocked his room and just kind of flopped down onto the bed. Just as his eyes closed he was awakened by the ringing of his cell phone. He picked it up hoping it'd be good news for a change.

"Hello?"

"Where you at Ray?"

"I don't think it'd be in my best interests to say."

"I understand. Someplace that you've never been to before I hope."

"Yeah, I've never been here before."

"That's good. It's unlikely he'll find you there then."

"Why's that?"

"Because both he and I know all the places that you've been known to go. Much more difficult to track you to an unfamiliar spot."

"You seem to know everything about him and how he thinks. How is that?"

"Because we're both from the same organization."

"Organization?"

"We fulfill contracts."

"You mean you're hitmen."

"You can call it anything you like; it all boils down to the same thing."

"So if you're both hitmen, why have you been warning me?"

"Because I don't want to see you killed. I was offered your contract first, but I turned it down. After turning it down I left the organization. I'm retired now, I've had enough. Maybe by saving you I can redeem myself in some small way."

"So why all the strange phone calls? Why don't you come out where I can see you or meet you?"

"Because that might endanger both of us. The best chance you have is by trying to avoid him and letting me try to track him down. If he were to see both of us together, both our lives wouldn't be worth a penny. He may be on to me already, I don't know."

"I guess I should thank you for warning me already. I'd probably be dead by now if you hadn't."

"Thank me when it's over. Anyway, you better rest up some. I'll call you in the morning."

"Wait, I have one more question."

"What is it?"

"Why was Stacy killed?"

The voices on the phone fell silent for a few minutes. The man on the other end wasn't sure if he was ready to handle the answer.

"I'll tell you tomorrow."

"Why not now?"

"Because you're tired and you've had a long difficult night. You'll think much more clearly in the morning after you've had some sleep."

"OK."

After hanging up with his newly found partner, Spencer turned on the TV to try and turn his attention away from his troubles. He hoped it'd be able to distract him till he was able to fall asleep. The commercials faded away and the late night movie, The Fugitive, started playing.

"How symbolic," he whispered.

He watched the movie and it seemed to take his mind off of things, helping him to relax a little. He fell asleep soon after that with thoughts of Stacy running through his mind. He wondered what it was about her that the voice on the phone didn't want to tell him just yet.

By this time the police had been called about Stacy's death. The FBI was called in to head the investigation. Bill Collins was to be in charge of the investigation along with his team of Marty Stewart and Nathan Scott. Collins arrived at the apartment complex with Stewart and Scott already there waiting for him with the area swarming with reporters and onlookers.

Collins was thirty-six years old and had been an agent for eleven years. He was very thorough, dedicated, and had a tendency to be sarcastic in a serious, but humorous way. He didn't stop till he accomplished what he was after. Stewart and Scott were younger men who were similar to Collins only not quite as serious minded. They had been agents for five and two years respectively.

Collins looked at all the commotion and shook his head in disgust. He liked to work on cases in a quiet manner without having to deal with the media.

"Would you look at all this," Collins stated. "It's like a bunch of sharks at a feeding frenzy who smell blood in the water."

"Murders are always good for ratings and selling papers," Stewart responded.

Once inside the apartment, Collins was led to the bedroom where Stacy's body was. He bent over the body to examine her a little more closely.

"Pretty. Alright, give it to me Nate."

"Stacy Hill, twenty-four years old, killed by what looks like a knife wound, worked at a jewelry store, no close relatives, has a boyfriend, been dead around two or three hours."

"Murder weapon?"

"Hasn't been found yet."

"Who found the body?"

"An anonymous tip."

"Oh, just love those," Collins joked sarcastically.

"Has to come from somewhere I guess."

"Boyfriend's name?"

"Ray Spencer."

"Has he been contacted?"

"No answer on his phone."

"You and Marty swing by where he lives and talk to him."

Collins continued throughout the apartment, looking for any clues to identify the killer. The place was remarkably clean and devoid of anything, other than the body, that would indicate a murder was committed there. He walked through the living room and noticed that the phone line was cut then turned and saw her cell phone lying on the floor. A half hour later he got a call on his cell phone.

"Collins here."

"Bill, it's Marty. We're at Spencer's house. I think you better get over here. We've got a knife with blood on it."

"Alright, get the appropriate people out there and I'll be there soon."

Stewart gave him the address to Spencer's house, and Collins spoke to the photographer briefly about the type of pictures he wanted before leaving. Upon arriving at Spencer's home, he saw more reporters hovering around it.

"Goddamn," he asserted as he got out of his car.

He maneuvered his way through the reporters on the way to the house. He answered no questions except for saying that he'd have a statement for them later. Stewart and Scott were waiting for him by the door.

"How the hell'd these reporters get here so fast?"

"Someone must've tipped 'em off," Stewart answered.

"Geez, they're like sharks…"

"At a feeding frenzy who smell blood in the water," Stewart continued for him.

"You think you're funny or something?"

"I always thought so, didn't you think so," he said, turning to Scott.

"Mildly amusing, anyway," Scott shot back.

"How'd you two clowns ever make it through the academy?"

"Well I cheated, and he made it through on sheer luck," Stewart remarked.

"I believe it. Alright, what's the story here, Martha Stewart, I mean Marty. Sorry."

"Ha ha, very funny. Asshole."

Collins looked around while grinning at the witty banter they were displaying towards each other.

"Anyway, not much to it here. Knife on the floor here, with some blood, upstairs bedroom's messed up a little, that's about it," Stewart said. "Oh yeah, there's also two bullet holes in there, one in the floor, one in the ceiling."

"Has the gun been found?"

"Not yet."

The agents proceeded to go up to the bedroom examining it for any evidence. They walked through the rest of the house not coming up with much in the way of clues. They stood in the living room talking about the case.

"OK, so what do we have here?" Collins asked.

"Woman killed with a knife in her apartment, knife and blood found at boyfriend's house, boyfriend is missing," Stewart responded.

"Sounds like an open and shut case. All we have to do is find Spencer," Scott chimed in.

"Don't be so quick to jump to the obvious answer," Collins said.

"C'mon Bill, the knife is in his house," Stewart replied.

"How do you know he wasn't shaving with it and cut himself?"

Collins lowered his head and put his hand over his forehead as he often did when he was deep in thought.

"If the knife is the murder weapon, then why are there two bullet holes upstairs?" Collins asked. "And why is the knife all the way down here, and not up there? And why is this knife even here? Wouldn't a logical man throw the damn thing away or even clean it off or something?"

Nobody seemed to have any answers to the questions Collins had posed. The three men stood silent for a few seconds before Collins spoke up again.

"OK, here's what we'll do. I'll make a statement saying Spencer is a suspect, but not necessarily the top suspect. He's not being charged, he's not wanted for anything right now other than questioning. Maybe if he thinks there's someone we want more than him, he'll be a little more lackadaisical in his movements. Nathan, I want you to check out Spencer's background. I want everything on him from the time he was sixteen. Where he went to school, what sports he played, who he's had sex with, you name it, I want it. Marty, make sure you have all the information about the crime scenes ready in the morning."

"No problem," Stewart answered.

"Also send out a picture and description of Spencer to every air-port, train station, bus station, and cab company in the area. If he goes somewhere, I wanna know where he's heading."

"Will do."

"OK, meet at the office at ten."

Collins went outside to make a statement to the press, while the other two agents scooted by them.

"What did he mean, not the top suspect? I thought he was our only suspect," Scott said sarcastically.

"C'mon you knucklehead," Stewart responded, giving him a play-ful shove in the shoulder.

3

Spencer was woken up in the morning by the sounds of the TV. He yawned and struggled to keep his eyes open when he heard the newscaster say something that peaked his interest. He perked his head up and rubbed the sleep from his eyes. They were talking about Stacy's death on the news. The picture cut away to some footage that was shot the previous night at Stacy's apartment.

"This was the scene last night at the Midtown Apartment Complex. The FBI is handling the investigation and have said that twenty-four year old Stacy Hill was murdered in her apartment last night, killed by a knife wound. A statement has been issued saying that the top suspect in Hill's death is twenty-six year old Ray Spencer".

A small picture of Spencer appeared in the top right hand corner of the screen. Spencer couldn't believe it. First he was almost killed, his girlfriend was murdered, and now he was a known fugitive. He kept on listening as the newscaster continued.

"Hill and Spencer had been dating for the last several months. Investigators searched Spencer's house early this morning trying to contact him about Hill's death. In searching Spencer's home, they found a blood-stained knife that is believed to be the murder weapon. The FBI warns that Spencer is considered armed and very dangerous. If you have any information regarding Spencer's whereabouts please call your local law enforcement authorities."

Spencer listened intently and hung onto every word that was said. He was almost paralyzed staring at the screen in a state of shock that they thought he killed Stacy. That must've been why he was told not to call the police. He would've been giving himself up. He could give himself up and explain his side of the story, but he had no proof to back it up. They already seemed to have the evidence they needed to pick him as the top suspect.

With thousands of people seeing that newscast Spencer would now have to be even more cautious than he was before. He put his hand over his head, depressed about the situation he found himself in. A few minutes later he got a phone call from the man who'd been helping him.

"I just saw on the news I'm the top suspect."

"Yeah, I saw it."

"Now what am I gonna do?"

"Don't lose your head. If you're gonna get out of this you'll have to remain calm and not panic."

"I can't stay here forever though. I'm going to have to try and clear myself."

"I'm working on getting evidence that'd clear you."

"I can't just sit here and wait though. What if something happens to you or you don't get it? What if him or the police show up?"

The man thought about it for a few seconds and quickly realized that Spencer was right.

"First, get yourself a gun just in case. You can't defend yourself against him without one. But don't use it unless you have no choice."

"How much do they cost?"

"Don't matter, buy it or steal it."

"I'm not gonna steal a gun."

"Right now you're wanted for murder, whether you steal a gun isn't going to make one bit of difference."

"OK."

"And if you're gonna go out and try to clear yourself, do it the right way."

"How's that?"

"Make yourself invisible."

"How do I do that?"

"Don't go anywhere you've been in the last month. Be careful about contacting anyone you know as they could turn you in whether they do it intentionally or not. After today, try not to go out in the daytime. Stick to moving at night, it's more difficult to spot you. The more people you avoid, the more you'll disappear."

"Got it."

"Good. One more thing, ditch your cell phone. The FBI will be able to trace you within a few days if you don't."

"Alright."

"I'll talk to you later then."

"What if I need to contact you for some reason? Where can I reach you?"

The man finally gave Spencer his name, Robert, and a number where he could be reached. He wondered if that was really his name or just an alias he used. Spencer thought if his face was going to be in the papers and on the news, it might be best if he stayed at a different place every night so nobody would get to look at him too often. He took a shower and was getting ready to go out when his phone rang again. He picked it up, but it was an unfamiliar voice that said his name.

"Who's this?"

"I didn't think you'd forget me so easily."

Spencer was numb thinking of who it was. He couldn't find any words to speak. The man spoke up again.

"Need a reminder?"

"I know who you are."

"Good. I underestimated you last night. You're much more difficult than I thought you'd be. I like a challenge though. Keeps a person on their toes."

"Why'd you kill Stacy? Why didn't you just stick to me?"

"I didn't kill her, you did."

"Cut the bullshit. Why'd you do it?"

"Because she got in over her head. You should be thanking me for that."

"Why would I do that?"

"Come on, Ray, even you should be able to figure it out."

"I'm gonna kill you," Spencer said in a brief moment of anger.

The man found that amusing and just laughed at the boldness of the statement.

"Are you? Then why are you hiding from me? I'll find you eventually. If I don't get you then the police will. Either way I win."

"Not if I get you first."

"I hope you get your chance."

"I will."

"I like your confidence. But if you're gonna kill me, do it for yourself, not for Stacy. She's not worth it."

"How would you know?"

"Ray, Ray, Ray. Who do you think set you up?"

Spencer was silenced. He would not believe this killer was being honest with him.

"It's true. She informed the company's executives what you were doing for a pretty nice fee. She sold you out. Only thing was she asked for more money and threatened to go public if she didn't get it. Dumb move, very, very dumb."

Spencer was still speechless. He was just letting the words hit him, bouncing off him.

"It wasn't how I intended it to be but it turned out for the best. See, since I didn't kill you, the best option was to kill her and blame it on you. Now you're both out of the picture."

"You could've killed me easily. Why'd you hide and wait till I got upstairs."

"Well if I killed you from a distance, the police would then figure it was premeditated and dive into all sorts of things and possibly find out your company's situation. By doing it up close, it makes it seem like a random killing. You caught a robber in the act, and it was your tough luck. Guess it's still gonna be your tough luck anyway."

"What makes you think I won't turn myself in to the police and tell them everything?"

"Because you have no proof. The briefcase you had that contained all the evidence you turned up is no longer in your possession. And if I hear that you turned yourself in voluntarily, I will eliminate your parents the same way that I did your girlfriend."

The man then hung up on Spencer's stunned ears. At least now he had some answers though. He wasn't completely in the dark about what happened and why. He still couldn't believe Stacy could do that though. He loved her so much, and she was willing to let him get killed for money. He wondered how he could've been so wrong about her. She never even gave any reason to suspect anything.

Rage grew within him and for the first time he didn't feel sorry that she was dead. She got what she had coming to her, he thought. There was nothing he could do about her now though. Now all he needed to think about was trying to stay alive, while also avoiding the police at the same time. He left his room, and walked down the hall with his head down so nobody would recognize him if they walked by. After slipping out of the hotel, his stomach told him he was starving, so the first thing Spencer decided to do was eat breakfast.

Spencer clung to the sides of buildings as he walked the streets, trying to make himself less noticeable. He got the feeling that somebody would notice him any minute, and the police were within seconds of closing in. He spotted a McDonald's and ordered some breakfast, which he took with him to a bench outside. He bought a paper from a stand and made sure it covered his face as he read it to prevent anybody from seeing him. There he was right on the front page of the news. He curiously read the article to see how he was presented in it. It seemed like they were basically saying he was guilty.

Collins was already in his office reading the paper when Stewart and Scott walked in.

"You guys read the paper or seen the news?" he asked them.

"Yeah, we've seen them," Scott answered.

"This is why I hate dealing with those people, they said he's the top suspect and we found a knife which we believe to be the murder weapon, I never said that," Collins said while tossing the paper down. "For once why don't they report what I say instead of twisting my words around to suit them?"

"What'd you say?" Stewart asked.

"I said he is a suspect and we found a knife which may or may not be the murder weapon."

Stewart handed Collins a cup of coffee while they discussed the case. Collins looked over a few papers before turning his attention to Scott.

"What you got for me Nathan?"

"As far as a criminal record goes, he has none. He doesn't own a gun either."

"So he's clean? No parking tickets, no untidy underwear, nothing?"

"He's cleaner than Telly Savalas' head on Kojak."

"Great, he's a regular boy scout."

"I talked to his parents this morning to find out a little more about him."

"What'd they say?"

"Played baseball and tennis in high school. Was a good student, had good grades. He worked two jobs while in college to pay for it."

"Parents couldn't help?"

"He wouldn't let them. He wanted to feel like he earned it himself."

"What do they do?"

"His father's a stockbroker and his mother's a doctor."

"My God he is a boy scout," Collins said turning to Stewart.

"Was," Stewart retorted.

"One thing's for certain, if he ever needs money, he'll never run out."

"Let's out guarding banks," Stewart remarked.

"What about the predicament he's got himself in right now?"

"Well they don't know where he's at and they haven't talked to him in over a month."

"Don't get along?"

"They get along very well. They said he told them he was working on something big and wouldn't be able to talk to them for a while cause it'd take up most of his time."

"Something big. What the hell could that be?"

"They also said he's not capable of killing someone. His mother said he was always the kind of person who if he saw an ant he'd be careful not to step on it."

"Well that's just fine and dandy except we're not looking for an ant killer. Marty, the next time we're looking for an ant killer remind me to scratch him off the list."

"Will do, chief."

"What about his relationship with Hill?"

"His parents said they seemed to love each other. Spencer never told them of any arguments or fights they had, so they assume everything was good between them."

Collins sat there thinking with his hand over his mouth tapping his lip with his middle finger.

"You got anything else for me?"

"That's it for me," Scott concluded.

"OK. Nate, get someone out there watching their house in case he tries to get in touch with them."

"You got it."

"Marty, did you get a picture and description out to the airport and other places?"

"Yeah, nothing's turned up on him though."

"What else you got for me?"

"Well the blood on the knife matches the victim. I also found out that it matches Spencer too, just thought I'd throw that in there for that shaving theory of yours."

"That was kind of you."

"It was, wasn't it?"

"What else?"

"Knife has Spencer's prints on it, which was found out by matching it to other prints we found throughout the house."

"What about the two bullet holes upstairs?"

"Made by a gun with a silencer on it."

Stewart then revealed a large envelope and placed it on Collins' desk. In it were pictures from the crime scenes and phone records of both Hill and Spencer.

"OK, let's go through it and see what we come up with," Collins stated.

The three of them looked through the pictures trying to notice if anything caught their eye. Collins found a couple that interested him and tossed it in Stewart's direction.

"Look at these."

"Pictures of the steps," Stewart said.

"The top, middle, and bottom. The top of the stairs are clean, but the middle and bottom have traces of blood on them, now how do you account for that?"

"He took some stain remover and cleaned the top of the steps?"

"This case isn't making any sense," Scott spoke up.

"Why's that?" Collins questioned.

"The blood on the stairs, and why would he drop the knife in his house? If he was gonna leave it, why didn't he leave it at her apartment?"

"Good thinking, I was hoping I wasn't the only one baffled by that."

The rest of the pictures didn't really lead to any interesting observations. They then started looking over the phone records.

"Spencer receives a call at 10:02, then nothing the rest of the night. Hill makes a call at 9:46, receives one at 10:18, receives another one at 10:30, and another one at 10:58," Stewart noted.

"You know, I don't think I'm gonna like this case very much," Collins said. "Do we know who they talked to on those phone calls?"

"The only one we know is the last one at 10:58 which came from The Sports Haven bar. The others were from phone booths in the area."

"Let's start with that one. Nathan, go talk to 'em, show them some pictures."

"What about cell phone records?" Collins asked.

"We should have them in a few days," Stewart told him.

Scott then left to see if Spencer had been seen at the bar, while the remaining agents went over some theories on the case.

"There's one more interesting thing," Stewart noted.

"What's that?" Collins asked.

"Hill was killed between eleven and twelve. I fooled around with the cell phone lying on the floor, checked out recent calls, and there was one received just after twelve."

"So the question is who took it, and who called."

"They did lift some prints off it, and it matched Spencer's. He was there around that time, too."

"Was the call from a pre-set number?"

"No, came up unavailable."

"Think out loud for me, Marty. Throw some stuff at me."

"Well I was thinking maybe she was stabbed at Spencer's, left, then eventually died at her place. But there was no blood anywhere else in her apartment or her car. You'd figure she'd have had some on her hand from dabbing at it to cover it up. That means she'd have got it on her steering wheel, doorknob, maybe drip some in her apartment. There's no evidence of that, so she was definitely killed instantly in her apartment."

"Which means Spencer would've been home at ten, went to her apartment after eleven, then went back to his house and dropped the knife. Why does that not make sense?"

They discussed things for a while longer trying to piece the evidence together, though they weren't coming up with many answers. They seemed to wind up with more questions then they started with. Scott called Collins not too long after that from the bar.

"Spencer was here last night."

"Who remembers him?"

"The bartender. He said he remembers him so well because of how wet he was. He came in totally soaked from the storm. As soon as he entered the bar, he used the phone, then went to the bathroom, came back out and had a drink."

"What time did he say that was?"

"Bout 10:30 or 11."

At that time, Stewart was notified that he had a phone call, so he left to take it.

"So we'll assume it was him that made that 10:58 phone call."

"Yeah, bartender also said Spencer told him his car broke down and he was walking, which is why he was so wet. He also said Spencer seemed out of it, like he was nervous or jumpy."

"OK, so if his car did break down, now all we have to do is go find it."

"Wait, that means if he was walking…" Scott started before Collins cut him off.

"Then that means he had a ride from there to her apartment."

Stewart came walking back in and hearing him talk about the car, interrupted Collins.

"They found it," Stewart told him. "Wilson elementary school."

"Nathan, they found Spencer's car. Find out if any buses or taxi's frequent that area, and if they do, talk to them and find out if they picked up someone matching Spencer's description and took him to Hill's apartment."

The agents left the office on their way to the school. They were now starting to put the events together. When Collins and Stewart arrived, the police officer that responded to the call filled them in. He told them that the principal called it in after the car had been sitting there all morning. The doors were unlocked and they searched the car but came up with nothing of interest, except the keys were still in the ignition. Collins took the keys out and took a brief look at the surrounding area. The two agents stood to the side of the car looking it over some more.

"You find it funny he left the doors unlocked?" Collins asked.

"What's the difference? If it's not working, nobody's gonna steal it," Stewart answered. "And there's nothing in it to steal."

"Could steal the radio. He didn't even take his keys with him," Collins noted as he tossed the keys to Stewart.

"Well if he was thinking about killing his girlfriend, then he wouldn't be thinking logically about this stuff."

"I wonder."

Collins turned his attention to the responding officer while grabbing the keys out of Stewart's hand.

"Anybody try to start this car?"

"No sir," the officer replied.

Collins then sat in the driver's seat, and put the keys back in the ignition. He turned the key and the car started immediately.

"Son of a bitch," Stewart said in surprise.

Collins climbed out of the car and looked at it with his arms crossed, deep in thought. He pulled out his phone and called Scott to see if he had any developments.

"A cab was at the bar around 11:30, Spencer got in and went to Hill's apartment complex. Spencer told him where to stop, he got out, came back about five or ten minutes later," Scott reported.

"He stop at Hill's apartment?"

"No, it was a row behind it."

"Then what?"

"Then he took him back to his house."

"Did you ask him if he noticed whether his car was there?"

"I did. He said there was a car in the driveway."

"He notice anything about Spencer? Actions, carrying anything?"

"Said he seemed kind of distant, but he wasn't carrying anything that he noticed."

"Good job, Nate. I want you to go talk to some of Hill's co-workers and friends, see what they got to say. Marty and I will take Spencer's."

Collins informed Stewart of what Scott found out and they mulled it over on the way to interviewing some of Spencer's colleagues. The first person on the list was Wilson Marcus, who was the accounting manager at Hartwell Enterprises. Collins said he'd talk to Marcus and told Stewart to talk to some of Spencer's co-workers. Collins was led to Marcus' office, and was told to wait there, and he'd be in shortly. Marcus walked in only a minute later. Collins introduced himself and started asking questions.

"What can you tell me about Ray Spencer?"

"He was hard working, intelligent, honest, an all-around nice guy."

"Do you know if he owned a gun?"

"Not that I am aware of. I've never heard him mention anything about guns."

"Ever meet his girlfriend?"

"Yes, I met her several times."

"And what'd you think of her?"

"She seemed to be a very nice woman. Did Spencer ever talk about any arguments they might have had or did you ever observe anything that now might seem kind of odd?"

Marcus briefly thought it over, going over situations in his mind.

"No," he said while shaking his head. "They seemed to be very happy."

"So what do you think about what happened?" Collins asked.

"It's certainly a horrible thing. It's all anyone's talking about to-day."

"Do you think he did it?"

Marcus thought about it for a few seconds before answering.

"No."

"Why not?"

"He's never struck me as the violent type."

"He told his parents he was working on something big that would take up a lot of his time. Do you know what he was talking about?"

"No, I really couldn't say. He wasn't working on anything of terrible importance here, just regular everyday stuff. It must've been something outside the office."

"Do you think he'd ever come to anybody here for help in eluding us?"

"I honestly don't know."

"Has anybody been in his office today?"

"Not to my knowledge."

"Good. I'm going to have to request that nobody enters his office. I'll have some people going through it to see what kind of evidence we can uncover."

"Of course. Anything you need."

Collins continued questioning him for another fifteen minutes about Spencer and the kind of work he did there. He really wasn't getting any answers that lead him any closer to finding him. After leaving Marcus, Collins searched Spencer's office. He wasn't looking for anything in particular though. He was just waiting for something to jump out at him, but nothing did. He looked through his desk, some files, fumbled around with the computer, but nothing that seemed out of the ordinary.

Collins left the office and met up with Stewart in the lobby of the building. Stewart told him that he talked to four of Spencer's co-workers, but nobody had anything bad to say about him, and nobody knew where he was.

"Get one of the computer experts to go through Spencer's machine. If we're lucky something will turn up that'll give us some indication about his next move, or where he's heading, or what he's thinking of doing," Collins said.

"Where to now?" Stewart asked.

"Back to the office so we can try and sort this out. Call Nathan and tell him to meet us there."

Collins and Stewart were in the office discussing matters when Scott walked in.

"Hope you found out more than we did," Collins said to him.

"I'll give you the short version…"

"In other words, he found out nothing," Stewart interrupted.

"Well?" Collins asked.

"Basically…I found out nothing," Scott confessed.

"If that don't beat all," Collins gushed.

"Everyone I talked to said she was a nice girl, Spencer was a nice guy, they seemed very much in love, and nobody knows where he's at."

"So what do we have here?" Collins asked. "Besides a whole lot of nothin'."

Collins looked at the picture of the knife found in Spencer's house, then looked at pictures of the steps. There was something about it that was troubling him, but he couldn't quite put his finger on it.

"Why would a guy walk through the pouring rain when his car was working?" Collins asked.

Nobody had an answer to the question.

"And why take a cab to kill the woman?"

"Maybe he didn't intend to kill her," Scott answered.

Collins continued looking at the picture of the knife when he finally figured out what it was that was bothering him.

"Is Spencer right or left handed?" he asked.

"Right," Stewart said.

"Look at the picture of the knife," Collins said, handing it to Stewart.

"What about it?"

"Hill was stabbed on her right side, correct?"

"Yeah, so?"

"So I don't think that's the murder weapon."

"How do you figure that?"

"For a right handed person to stab someone on their right side, they'd have to be behind them. There'd be an awful lot of blood as there was by the body. That knife is not covered in blood; it's only on a small portion of it. And on the steps, it looks smeared, not like it was dripping."

"Maybe the rain washed it off the knife," Stewart responded.

"Cab driver said he wasn't carrying anything."

"Maybe he had it in his pocket or something."

"Then why the smeared blood on the steps?"

Stewart gave out a deep, frustrating sigh.

"I hate this case," he muttered.

"What? Just starting to get interesting now," Collins said with a slight smile. "There's something else bothering me about the way she was killed."

"What's that?" Stewart wondered.

"She was killed from behind right?"

"Yeah, we've established that."

"So if you kill someone you know with a knife, don't you do it facing them? That should put the wound on the opposite side. Usually strangers kill from behind to get the element of surprise."

"Don't even tell me you don't think he did it," Stewart said.

"I'm not saying that. I'm just pointing out other possibilities. There's no question all the evidence points to him."

"So is he still our top suspect?" Scott asked.

"He better be, he's the only one we've got," Collins said.

"He did it, otherwise he wouldn't have disappeared," Stewart stated.

"Unless he was kidnapped, or dead too," Collins shot back.

"Wait, if that's not the murder weapon, then whose blood is it and what's the knife doing there?"

"Spencer's. He was walking down the stairs, shaving, and fell down the steps. He cut himself smearing blood on the steps and left the knife. Bingo, my shaving theory was accurate," Collins said with a clap of his hands, laughing like he'd just won a bet.

"I should've listened to my uncle and became a barber," Stewart remarked.

"Good idea, then Spencer wouldn't have cut himself going down the steps. You'd have saved me all the stress on this case," he said with another laugh.

"Anybody ever tell you you're impossible?" Stewart asked.

"No," Collins mocked, like he was surprised to be called that.

The three of them came to the conclusion that the knife they found was not the murder weapon. They couldn't figure out why he left his car originally and then came back for it. They also had yet to find a motive for why Spencer would kill his girlfriend.

"Just to be sure, get the lab working on whether that knife could've been used to kill her or whether it was a bigger or smaller knife that did it."

"I'll get on it," Stewart said.

"We've still yet to account for those two bullet holes," Collins stated.

"I've got something," Scott proclaimed.

"Let me hear it," Collins responded.

"Suppose Spencer intended to kill her in his house. Gets a gun, puts a silencer on it so nobody hears the shots. He goes upstairs to kill her. She's tough though and struggles with him, messing up the bed, firing off a couple shots. She throws a lamp at him and finds a knife on the table. She runs downstairs, but he catches her, with the knife wounding Spencer. She leaves; he drops the knife to follow her. His head's so messed up he just walks to the bar, not paying attention to the rain and decides he's gonna go kill her and does it."

Collins had his hand over his mouth and chin thinking about Scott's theory, letting it sink in. His eyes glanced over to Stewart, who gave him a look as if the theory was possible.

"I'm not sure if I buy that. It's possible," he said looking at Scott. "But there's some holes in that too, like every other theory we got. First, nobody reported seeing Spencer with blood on him. But it's something to keep in mind. Good thinking Nate."

"Thanks."

"Well, I don't think we're gonna solve this case till we find our boy," Collins told his men.

"He could be anywhere by now," Scott said.

Collins thought for a few minutes to figure out what their next move would be. They had no leads as to where they'd find Spencer, so they'd have to hope they got lucky.

"If he didn't sleep at home last night, that means he slept some- where else right?" Collins asked, though not really needing an answer.

"Maybe he slept in his car," Stewart said.

"Too risky. Sleeping in his car on the street, cop pulls up and he's done. No, he had to go somewhere."

"A hotel."

Collins shook his head in agreement.

"Nathan, go check any hotels, motels, or anyplace that puts people up for a night that's within twenty minutes of where that school is. If he was walking, he wouldn't have walked too far."

"Bill, we don't even have an idea of where to look for him or where he's going. He could take a plane, train, cab, bus or hitchhike to anywhere," Stewart told him.

"So let's find him."

4

As Spencer kept walking he made sure to stay out of open spaces. He tried to stay near trees, buildings, cars, whatever could conceal him. He came across a small shopping strip, and at the end of it was a little gun shop. He looked in the window, but didn't notice anyone inside. Spencer then saw a sign on the door, which gave the store's hours. It didn't open for another forty-five minutes.

Spencer nervously looked around to see if he was being watched. Being so early in the day though, there weren't many people around. He looked around for something he could use to smash the window of the door. He saw a good-sized stick laying on the ground, good enough to get the job done. Spencer grabbed it and smashed the glass just above the handle of the door. He reached his hand through the broken glass and unlocked the door. He was a little surprised at how easy it was. He figured a gun shop would be protected a little bit more.

Spencer rushed into the store and went to one of the gun cases. He had never held a gun before, and didn't even know anything about them. He picked one out and held it in his hand, getting the feel of it, and within minutes had the gun loaded. He shoved some extra ammunition into his pockets and put the gun inside the back of his pants, with his shirt covering it, and hastily left the store. It was the first criminal act that he'd ever done.

Now he needed to figure out where he was going. He couldn't just walk around aimlessly. Spencer had to determine what he was going to do, and how he was going to clear himself. He couldn't just wait around for Robert to come up with something, as he still wasn't totally certain he could trust him. He also needed to get a car. The more he walked, the more he was out in the open, anybody could see him.

Spencer thought about stealing a car but then the police would be on the lookout for a stolen car too. If he decided to hitchhike everywhere he went, somebody would eventually recognize him. He started walking down the highway with his face tucked in to his chest to prevent anybody recognizing him as they rode by. There weren't a lot of cars on the road but it was beginning to pick up a little.

Not too long after he began walking, looking out of the corner of his eye, Spencer noticed a black car slowing down as it went by. His eyes peered up to see that it stopped at the side of the road just ahead of him. He stopped and stared at the car trying to notice the driver. The windows were tinted though so he wasn't able to see who was inside. He'd never seen the car before so it definitely wasn't anybody he knew who happened to recognize him walking. It didn't appear that the car was having any problems since the driver wasn't getting out. It must've been sitting there waiting for him.

Spencer cautiously approached the car. He slipped his hand across his back, gripping his gun in case he had to use it. As he got close to the passenger side door, the window suddenly rolled down half way. He lowered his head to look inside the car and saw an attractive woman sitting there. She greeted him with a warm, friendly voice.

"Need a lift?" the woman asked.

Spencer hesitated slightly, taking a quick look to the back seat to make sure it was clear.

"Sure."

"Hop in," she said with a smile.

Spencer took his hand off his gun and stepped inside the car.

She reached her hand over to Spencer and introduced herself.

"I'm Samantha."

Spencer gave her a slight smile, shook her hand and introduced himself as well.

"I'm Ray."

As soon as he said his name he wondered if he should've said something else. He said it without thinking that she might be able to put the name and face together. It crossed his mind, however, that maybe she was one of those people who doesn't pay much attention to the news. She didn't seem to recognize him at first glance.

"Car trouble?" she asked.

Spencer was looking out the window kind of in a daze and didn't hear the question fully.

"Huh?"

"You were walking, have car trouble?"

"Oh, yeah."

"So where are you heading?"

"Umm, actually I was just kind of walking. I wasn't really going anyplace in particular. Didn't expect anybody to give me a lift."

"Where do you live, maybe I can take you home?"

"No, that's OK, I wouldn't want to take you out of your way."

"It wouldn't be a problem. I have the day off so I'm just running some errands."

Samantha seemed to be a very friendly woman. She was very attractive too. She had brown hair, a pretty face, and a good figure. Spencer thought to himself that most guys would love to be picked up by a girl like her. He'd have gladly traded his spot next to her to be out of the trouble he was in though. Spencer finally came up with an answer for her as to where she could drop him off.

"You know, you can just go to wherever you need to go, and I'll get out then."

"Sure."

"You've been very nice though. I do appreciate you giving me a ride."

She looked over at him and smiled. It was the kind of smile that could melt a man's heart.

"You're welcome. I try to be nice and do the right thing. If I was stranded or walking, I'd be thankful somebody stopped and offered to help, so I figured I should do it for someone else."

They drove a few minutes longer without saying anything to each other. Samantha was growing intrigued by the man she had just picked up. He was good looking, seemed nice, but she thought he seemed a little distant and nervous. He wasn't hitting on her or making passes at her, which was a nice change from most guys she had met lately.

"So what do you do?" Samantha asked.

"I'm an accountant."

As soon as he answered, Spencer turned his head as though he was disgusted with himself. He thought he should've lied and said something else, but his mind was blank. He was never a good liar though. She was probably bound to ask more questions about his work and she'd figure it out anyway.

"How bout you?"

"Oh, I work in real estate. Nothing terribly exciting but it pays the bills."

Samantha saw a 7-11 coming up and decided to pull in to the parking lot. She parked the car and wondered if it'd be the last she'd see of him. He seemed like the kind of guy she'd like to go out with sometime if he was interested.

"Well, I need some coffee, would you like anything while I'm in there?"

"No thanks."

"Will you be here when I get back?"

"Well, I should really get going."

"How bout lunch?"

Spencer started to hesitate in answering but was cut off before he had a chance to say no.

"C'mon, what else do you have to do?"

He thought it over and figured he might as well. Maybe he wouldn't be as easy to locate if he was with someone else.

"OK, I'll wait."

"Great, I'll be right back."

Spencer watched her as she walked into the store and got some coffee. She grabbed his attention when she glanced down at the newsstand as she walked past and picked up a paper. He'd be right on the front page for her to see. She didn't seem to look too closely at it as she checked out, but she'd notice it soon enough.

Spencer looked down to the ignition but the keys were gone. He decided not to chance sitting there so he got out of the car and started walking around to the side of the store. Samantha walked out of the store and noticed that Spencer was no longer in the car. She looked around to see if she saw him anywhere but he was nowhere in sight. She was a little disappointed that he didn't stick around.

As soon as Samantha sat in her car she took a sip of her coffee and glanced at the front page headlines. There he was on the front page. The man she had picked up and was just talking to was declared the top suspect in a murder. She could hardly believe what she was reading. He certainly didn't seem the violent type, but that would explain why he seemed nervous and distant. She kept reading and thought she should call the number that was listed for information in capturing him.

Spencer had just emerged from the side of the building when he noticed a police car pulling in from the other entrance. He quickly turned around and went back behind the side of the building. He noticed that Samantha's car was still sitting there so he headed straight for it. She didn't see him coming, still deep in reading about him. She snapped her head up in surprise when she heard the passenger door open and saw him get back in.

Spencer saw that she had a frightened look in her eyes and she started squirming a little. There was no doubt that she had read the story. He had to make sure that she wouldn't make a scene with a police car pulling in. He looked over and saw the police car coming around.

"Drive. Now," he forcefully said.

She hesitated slightly so Spencer pulled out the gun he was carrying. He didn't want to point it at her and make her even more nervous or have it accidentally go off, so he just pointed it at the floor, letting her know he had one. After the initial shock of seeing the gun she pulled out of the parking lot and started driving. He rubbed his eyes, wondering what kind of mess he'd gotten himself into now. He picked up the paper and took a deep sigh while looking at it before tossing it back down. He looked over at Samantha, and after seeing the scared look on her face, put the gun in his belt.

"I'm not gonna hurt you. You mustn't try anything though. As soon as I figure out what I'm gonna do I'll be out of your life."

"Where am I driving to?" she said with tears building up in her eyes.

Spencer saw a tear run down her face and guilt overrode him. It was exactly what he was trying to avoid. He didn't want to involve and endanger innocent people. He then figured what he needed to do was just stick in one spot for a little while.

"Are you married?" he asked.

"No."

"Do you live alone? Kids, dog, roommate, anything?"

"No."

"Drive to your place."

As soon as he said that, Samantha shot him a terrified look. Spencer wished there was something he could do to make her believe that she'd be alright but he knew there was nothing he could say. They arrived at her house within ten minutes. It was a small one-floor house as the rest of the neighborhood was. They got out of the car and walked up to the house with Spencer cautiously looking around for any signs of danger.

Once inside the house, Samantha sheepishly took a seat on the sofa. She tried to be careful in anything she did or said so as not to make Spencer angry or violent. Spencer took a look around the house to make sure there were no unexpected surprises waiting for him. After he was done searching the house he came back to the living room where Samantha was. He wanted to try and relieve some of her fears if he could.

"I didn't do it."

She didn't believe him, but she didn't want to say that in fear of angering him.

"You don't believe that, do you?" he asked.

Samantha just gave a slight shrug of her shoulders, not really knowing what to say. Spencer knew he had to try and convince her that he was innocent. He couldn't hurt her, but he didn't want her calling the police after he was gone. He also knew that the whole world thought he was guilty now; he wanted someone to believe in his innocence, even if it was only one person. Spencer dejectedly turned his head away wondering what he could do to change her mind about him. He then saw the phone and an idea came to him.

He picked up the cordless phone and held it out for Samantha to grab. She wondered what he was up to, but she took hold of it.

"Call the police," he told her.

"What?" she said in a surprised tone. She thought maybe she had misheard him.

"If you think I did it then call the police. I won't stop you."

All Samantha could muster was a confused look on her face. She didn't think there was any way he could be serious about that. Surely he was playing some kind of trick on her. She looked at the digits on the phone before glaring at the gun Spencer had tucked in his belt. She thought that if she started to dial he would stop her. Spencer saw that Samantha glanced at his gun so he took it out of his belt.

Spencer held the gun out and then flipped it up, catching the barrel. He then took Samantha's hand and placed the gun in it. She loosely gripped the gun, not very sure what to do with it, since she had never held one before. Spencer just looked at her stoically.

"I've given you the phone and the gun. The next move's yours."

Spencer stood there looking at her, not making a move in any direction. Samantha didn't say a word, not sure of what she felt. Her instincts were telling her to believe him, but if he was being truthful, how could everyone else be so wrong? Spencer could tell by her hesitations she was having doubts in her mind about what to believe.

"I don't know what else I can do to make you believe me."

Samantha finally put the phone down beside her, and let the gun slip out of her hand, falling to the floor. She felt that if he wasn't innocent, he wouldn't be trying so hard to convince her that he was, since he'd have nothing to gain out of it. Spencer gave her a little smile showing her he was relieved.

"So what happened?" Samantha asked.

"It's kind of a long story."

"Well, it looks like I've got the time."

Spencer spent the next little while explaining everything that happened. He spared no details, recanting everything as if he'd been through it a hundred times over.

"Why don't you go to the police and tell them what happened?"

"Why would they believe me? I have no evidence to support anything I say. They found a knife with blood on it, and they know I was at her apartment around the time she died. There's no proof of there being anyone else involved."

Spencer wondered how much longer it'd take for the investigators to catch up with him. He didn't think he'd be able to stay ahead of them for too long. His paranoia was telling him they were just around the corner.

Collins was walking to his office when he ran in to Stewart. Stewart told him that Scott had called, saying that he found where Spencer stayed at the night before.

"He checked in under the name Bob Smith," Stewart informed.

"Bob Smith, that's original. Clever too."

"He's an accountant, what do you expect? You know how dry and boring those people are."

"Nate get anything else?" Collins asked.

"No, Spencer slipped out early this morning through a side entrance."

"That figures."

"At least we know he's still somewhere in the area."

They walked into his office and Collins noticed a video tape sitting on his desk.

"What's this?" he asked, picking it up.

"Just came in a minute ago. Don't know what's on it though. They just said it had to do with the case."

Collins handed it to Stewart and told him to pop it in the VCR. Collins leaned back in his chair as the tape started playing. Once the picture became clear Collins leaned forward paying close attention to what he was seeing.

"Is that not our boy?" Collins asked.

"That's him."

They were looking at a videotape of Spencer stealing a gun from earlier that morning. They replayed it a few more times.

"What'd he go and do that for?"

"Why not? He's got nothing to lose. He's already facing a murder charge so what's it matter if he steals something?" Stewart replied.

"But he's already got a gun."

"Maybe he lost it or something. Or maybe he just wants a little extra backup."

"Why a gun? Why not a car?"

"Maybe the car's next," Stewart said with a shrug. "I dunno; I'm not really following along with his thinking pattern here."

"You don't steal a gun unless you intend on using it. The question now becomes who's the next target."

"Maybe he got it for protection."

"Against what?" Collins asked.

"Maybe us."

"If that's the reason then he won't let himself be taken easily. We may have to take him down."

"What if he got it to kill someone else?"

"Then we better find him before another body pops up," Collins stated.

"If he's gunning for somebody, you'd figure it has to be someone close to him. His parents are already being watched, which leaves someone from work."

"As good a place to start as any. Where is the gun shop located in reference to that hotel he stayed in last night?"

"It's a little ways east of there," Stewart informed him.

"Well if he continues in that direction that would put him on course with the Hartwell Enterprises building, would it not?"

"Yeah."

"Alright, get somebody out there to watch over the building. Also find out who he worked closely with that lives nearby. I have a feeling that if he's looking for someone, he'll be waiting for them."

"What makes you think he's heading for the Hartwell building?" Stewart wondered.

"I'm just guessing, Marty. We don't really have any other options right now so that's as good a place to start as any. If we're lucky, he'll turn up."

Collins got up out of his chair and walked over to the window. He just stared into the city, thinking about the case.

"What the hell are you doing, Ray," he said softly.

5

Spencer wound up spending the night at Samantha's house. He woke up on the couch with a blanket overtop of him. He didn't remember falling asleep there, but after the last couple days he was surprised he could still remember his own name. He sat up and instinctively looked around for Samantha but he didn't see her. He sat motionless trying to hear any noises that she was making so he could pick up where she was.

"Samantha?" he yelled out.

He waited for an answer but there was none coming. He went into the kitchen, the bedroom, and even the bathroom, but there was no sign of her. Spencer rushed over to the window to see if her car was still parked in the driveway, but it was gone.

"Damn," he cried.

Spencer wondered where she had gone. He didn't hear her leaving so she must've snuck out quietly. Since he was unsure of where she went, he didn't think he could stick around any longer. He thought she believed his story but he couldn't chance her coming back with the police any minute.

He looked around for his gun but he didn't see it anywhere. Spencer went over to the couch and checked under the pillow and between the cushions. He came up with nothing though. He reached his hand under the couch thinking that maybe it somehow slipped underneath it but it wasn't there either.

Spencer then checked the rest of the room with similar results. He tried the kitchen, and the bedroom, but it was nowhere to be found. He figured that Samantha must've taken it with her. He was starting to think that, once again, he'd been fooled by a woman.

He stood in the living room thinking of his next move when his ears were startled by the turning of the doorknob. Spencer raced over behind the door as it opened up. Standing behind the door quietly, careful as to not alert the person entering of his presence, he eagerly awaited whomever it was to walk in. He wondered what he'd use to defend himself since his gun was gone. The door opened slowly, as if the person was trying not to make any noise to sound off their being there.

The door opened three quarters of the way but nobody stepped into sight. Spencer wondered what they were waiting for. He saw the outline of someone emerge and he quickly pushed the door closed, ready to pounce on the unsuspecting intruder. The person was startled by the shutting of the door and turned around. Spencer was somewhat relieved to find that it was Samantha. He looked out the window to check if she brought company, but everything was clear. She could tell he was a little nervous and jumpy.

"Thought I was turning you in?"

"It crossed my mind," Spencer replied.

"I've trusted you. Why don't you try trusting me?"

"Well when I wake up and you're not here, and my gun's gone, what did you expect me to think? After what I've been through, I'm not too trustful of anyone right now."

"I'm sorry. I should've left a note for you or waited till you woke up."

"Well, I'm glad what I was thinking didn't turn out to be true."

"I was hoping to get back before you woke up. I bought stuff for breakfast," she said, holding up a bag of groceries. "I was planning to go to the store yesterday, but someone interrupted my plans."

"What'd you take my gun for?"

"Cause I didn't want to take a chance on maybe surprising you and you being trigger happy when I got back."

"Do I look trigger happy?"

She looked him up and down and simply shrugged with a coy smile. Spencer couldn't help but smile back at her.

"So do you trust me a little more now?" Samantha asked.

Spencer just slightly nodded his head indicating that he did. They walked into the kitchen where Samantha proceeded to make the two of them breakfast. As they finished eating their eggs they started talking about how he was going to clear himself.

"I don't even know where to start," Spencer said.

"Don't get frustrated. If you're going to get out of this you need to think clearly and calmly."

"Yeah, I know."

"Sounds to me like there's two places to start out with," Samantha noted. "The Hartwell Enterprises building for any documents regarding the accounting errors, and the house of whoever's in charge of the cover-up."

"That'd be Wilson Marcus."

"So I'd imagine he must keep some statements, or anything that would indicate what's going on. So that's a beginning."

"Yeah, but they've gotta be expecting me to show up somewhere. It'd be risky going to either place. The police might be staking out both places, and that doesn't include this guy who's trying to kill me. Who knows where he is or where he'll show up next."

"It's risky not going there. It's the only chance you have. You can't just sit around and wait for a miracle to pop up."

"I guess that's true."

"We'll figure out a way."

"What do you mean, we?" Spencer asked.

"You don't think I'm going to just let you do it all yourself, do you?"

Spencer just shook his head no like there was no chance of him letting her come with him.

"C'mon, you know you can't do it alone. You need help."

"No, I can't let you get involved."

"I'm already involved. I'm harboring a fugitive."

"Yeah, but…"

"But nothing, don't be stubborn. You asked me to believe in you, and I have, so let me help."

"What about your work?"

"Don't worry; I can take care of that."

"I have a feeling you won't take no for an answer."

"You can say no if you want to. But I'll just call the police after you leave if you do."

"Are you blackmailing me?"

"If that's what you want to call it."

"There are laws against that you know."

"Wanna call a cop?" Samantha said sarcastically.

"I knew I shouldn't have hitchhiked."

"So where do you wanna go first?"

"Might as well start at Wilson Marcus' house."

Spencer and Samantha then left, on their way to the home of Marcus. They continued talking along the way, both feeling more comfortable with each other as the minutes passed by. In what seemed like no time at all, they'd arrived at Marcus' home. They both looked up and down the street, trying to spot anything that looked suspicious. Everything seemed to be normal. Spencer told Samantha to stay in the car with it running in case he had to come out in a hurry.

As Spencer walked up to the house he felt very anxious. He hoped he could find something in Marcus' house that'd help to clear him. He'd been invited to the house before so he already knew his way around it. Spencer walked around to the back of the house where there was a sliding glass door. He noticed a small rock in the lawn, and picked it up, throwing it against the door. The glass shattered upon impact. Once Spencer entered he headed straight for the office where Marcus worked, but he was also mindful to be aware of everything around him. He couldn't be sure of where his attacker would turn up next.

Looking through the drawers of Marcus' desk, Spencer didn't notice anything of special interest. He turned the computer on and began looking through some of the files that were on it trying to come up with something. That also turned out nothing of interest. Spencer quickly looked through the rest of the house. He didn't want to stay there too long though. After half an hour of searching he determined that he wasn't going to find anything. Once he got back to the car he informed Samantha that he didn't turn up anything. They went back to her house to figure out their next course of action.

Wilson Marcus had gone back to his house about 1 o'clock to eat lunch. He noticed the police swarming around his house as he pulled into the driveway. As soon as he was informed that his house was broken into he checked to see if anything was missing. He knew it had to have been Spencer.

Collins was sitting at his desk when Stewart walked in with the news.

"What do you look so chipper about?" Collins asked.

"The house of Wilson Marcus was illegally entered sometime this morning."

"Do we know who?"

"A neighbor spotted a man coming out of the house and gave a description that matches Spencer. I figure we'll show him a picture as soon as we get out there to get a positive ID."

"Quite an interesting development."

"Not quite as interesting as one other thing."

"What's that?" Collins asked, leaning back in his chair with his hands clasped behind his head.

"According to the witness, Spencer hopped into a black car upon leaving. He doesn't know what kind it was or the license plate number either."

"So he finally stole himself a car."

"Not necessarily. Spencer was in the passenger side."

"Who the hell was driving?"

"We don't know. The man could only tell that it was a woman and she had blonde hair," Stewart said with a shrug.

"Now we gotta start looking for someone else too…damn. Call Nate and tell him to meet us there. Tell him to talk to that witness before we get there."

"You got it."

Collins and Stewart arrived about thirty minutes later. Once they got there, they noticed Scott, who informed them that the man did identify the picture of Ray Spencer as the same guy who came out of the house. Collins told Scott to check on any stolen cars matching the description of the car that Spencer got in. Once Collins noticed Marcus walking on the lawn he proceeded to ask him a few questions.

"Mr. Marcus, mind answering some questions?"

"Not at all, Agent Collins."

"Sorry about your house," Collins stated, as he looked the house over.

"I guess it shows that nobody is immune to criminal acts."

"Have any idea who might be responsible?"

"Isn't that your job? Your guess is as good as mine."

"Guessing would be a waste of time considering we both know who it was."

"Who would that be?"

"I don't think you're really that stupid, Mr. Marcus."

"What makes you think it was Ray?"

"Well, considering most professional burglars wouldn't throw a rock through a glass door to get in, and nothing of value was taken, that kind of makes it obvious," Stewart answered. "That and someone saw him come out."

"So if he didn't take anything, then what was the point of him breaking in?"

"He was looking for something," Collins informed him.

"Such as?"

"You tell us, Mr. Marcus. He went through your desk and your computer. You have something he wants. What would that be?"

"I assure you that I don't have any idea what it is he might be after."

There was a brief pause among the three men before Marcus spoke up again.

"What if Ray wasn't here looking for something, but to kill me like his girlfriend?"

"Who said he killed his girlfriend?" Collins asked.

"You did. Yesterday in my office…" Marcus stated before being interrupted by Collins.

"I did? I didn't say that. You just said that, I wouldn't have said that. Would I have said that?" he asked Stewart.

"No, I don't think you would've."

"I've never said whether I thought he killed his girlfriend or not, Mr. Marcus."

"What would he wanna kill you for?" Stewart asked.

"Like I said before, that's your job," he answered with a shrug.

"No, if he wanted to kill you, he'd have done it. He knows your work schedule, so he knew you wouldn't be home. If you were his target, right now we'd be investigating a homicide…your homicide, instead of an illegal entry. Spencer was definitely looking for something, Mr. Marcus, something you have," Collins stated while pointing at Marcus.

"I don't have anything that would interest him that I'm aware of. Sorry I can't be of more help."

"Any idea where he might be heading next?" Stewart asked.

Marcus simply shrugged his shoulders without saying a word.

"Well, be on the lookout. No telling where he'll turn up next," Collins informed him.

"He wouldn't come back here again, would he? I mean, I obviously don't have whatever it is that he's looking for, so there's no need for him to bother me, right?"

"Well, I'll let you in on a few new developments. As of this morning, he's now in possession of a car, a stolen gun, and an accomplice. So if he's after someone, I surely wouldn't want to be in their shoes."

Collins and Stewart finished with Marcus, and continued talking on the way to the car. A few reporters rushed up to Collins peppering him with questions about the case.

"Has it been determined whether Ray Spencer was responsible for the break-in?" one reporter asked.

"No comment," Collins answered.

"Any new developments in the case?" another reporter questioned.

"No comment," Collins once again bristled.

"Are you any closer to finding Spencer?" asked another reporter.

"No comment."

The agents then turned around to face the onslaught of reporters.

"Guys, as of right now, I have nothing new to report on any front of the investigation. When I have something of interest I will release a statement to you. Thanks for coming," Collins said as he promptly turned his back to the group.

"You'll give it to them, alright," Stewart remarked.

"God I hate these people. Vultures."

They continued walking undisturbed until they reached the car.

"Get someone to keep an eye on Marcus, Marty."

"Why, think Spencer will be back?"

"I'm not sure. There's just something about him. I don't trust him. He reminds me of the car salesmen who sold me my first car when I was 18."

"Why, what'd he do?"

"Car broke down two weeks after I bought it."

Both men had a laugh at the comparison.

"Sure that was a good idea telling him about the new developments?" Stewart asked.

"I think this guy's involved in something. I'm hoping what I told him might worry him a little and make something happen here."

They headed back to the office to work on the case. A short time after they arrived at the office Scott met them with the list of stolen cars from the previous day. Nothing that matched the car seen in front of Marcus' house was on the list though. Collins then had a call on his phone.

"Collins here. Right. Yeah. No question about it? OK. Thanks."

"What's up?" Stewart asked.

"They just analyzed the knife at Spencer's house. Not the murder weapon."

"How'd they figure that?"

"Hill's wound was made by a knife with a bigger blade. Didn't find any tissue or DNA on the knife that matched Hill either."

"Figures," Stewart sighed.

"No big deal. We already knew it wasn't the murder weapon anyway so it doesn't throw a wrench into our thinking at all."

"Yeah, but it would've been nice. Why can't things ever go smoothly?"

"Because the world is not a smooth place," Collins remarked.

"I guess it's back to the drawing board."

"Yep. That's the way the cookie crumbles."

Stewart just looked over to Scott, before looking back at Collins.

"Where do you come up with all these original sayings?" Stewart asked, his question dripping with sarcasm.

"Just pop up into my head, you know? Just occur to me. You have to be quick witted and thinking in this job," he said pointing at his temple.

"Unbelievable," Stewart replied.

"Yeah, well, I've been at this job longer than you. You stick around a few more years and you'll probably be able to come up with witty and original sayings just like me."

"I can't wait. Next thing we know you'll be saying, "you can't have your cake and eat it too," or "you can't cry over spilt milk"."

"All good sayings too."

"I'm sure you think so. Whoever came up with this stuff anyway, that Confucius guy?"

"Who?" Scott asked.

"I dunno, wasn't that some philosopher in India or something a few thousand years ago?"

"Got me."

"Alright, can we get back to the case here, Darwin?" Collins sarcastically asked Stewart.

"I guess if we have to."

Collins smiled as he shuffled a few papers around on his desk. They began throwing around more ideas about the case.

"Why does someone who's a suspect in a murder case disappear?" Collins asked.

"Because he's guilty and doesn't want to go to jail," Scott answered.

"Right. So why is he still in the area? Why hasn't he run?"

"Because he knows that's what we'd be looking for. He figures he'll stay low for a while, let things blow over, then move on," Stewart responded.

"But he's not staying low. By breaking into Marcus' house he's keeping himself visible, he's keeping the heat on, especially with someone that's close to him. Question is, why?"

"Cause he's looking for something," Stewart said, saying what was obvious.

"The man's wanted for murder, what would be so important?"

"Money. He needs it to keep himself afloat," Scott answered.

"Nah, it's not money. He could find any house that looks promising enough to hold valuable stuff, he didn't need to pick that one. Besides, he could always go to his parents for money.""Maybe he figures we'd be watching his parents house," Stewart said.

"He went to that house specifically looking for something that's important to him."

"Maybe Marcus is holding some document that would incriminate him in the crime also. Maybe Spencer figures if he goes down, he'll take Marcus with him. Or maybe he'll use that information if he's ever caught to make a deal on a lighter sentence," Stewart said.

"I'm not sure if I believe he's stupid enough to believe he'd get a lighter sentence, but the rest of that theory isn't bad. I'm telling you Marcus smells crooked."

"What if Marcus and Spencer are working on something, something big, his girlfriend finds out about it, threatens to turn them in, so they pop her," Stewart theorized.

"Hey, right now, I'm willing to accept anything," Collins stated. "There's one more thing we have to think about though."

"What's that?"

"The blonde. Where's she fit in this?"

"Not much we can do about that until we get some kind of info on her though. Right now we don't have anything on her."

"I know, but has she been in it with him all along, or is she a new recruit?"

"Things would make a little better sense if she was in it from the beginning. He finds a new girl to help him get rid of the old girl."

"I don't think we've seen the last of the surprises in the case."

6

Spencer and Samantha were watching a news report talking about the break-in of Wilson Marcus' house. The report mentioned that although authorities were not releasing details, it was widely assumed that Ray Spencer was involved. It also mentioned that Spencer was believed to be in the company of a blonde woman.

"What now?" Samantha asked.

"I don't know," Spencer sighed.

Spencer put his head in his hands and let out another loud sigh. It seemed that with every passing minute he was getting pulled in deeper. He started thinking again about what Robert told him about not trusting anyone. He looked at Samantha out of the corner of his eye.

"How far do you want to go with this?"

"What do you mean?" Samantha asked.

Spencer hesitated for a second, choosing his words carefully.

"With every move I make, I get deeper and deeper into trouble. First it was murder, then it was theft of a gun, now illegal entry. In order to clear myself, I may have to do a lot more."

"I know."

"Nobody knows anything about you; you can walk away from this now, still clean. If you continue on, and I can't clear myself, you'll go down with me."

"I know," she said slightly nodding.

"What makes you believe in me so much? I haven't even known you a week."

"I've been in a lot of bad relationships, Ray, and I've known a lot of bad people. There's a sincerity about you that I've never seen before in anyone else. I trust you."

She then gave him a hug and a kiss on the cheek.

"You can count on me," she told him. "Where are we going next?"

"The only other place is the Hartwell Enterprises building."

"When do you want to go?"

"Well it'll be dark in a few hours, so we might as well wait till then. Robert told me to stick to darkness as much as possible."

Samantha started making dinner for them when Spencer's cell phone started ringing. It became a sound that Spencer despised hearing. Every time he answered it he seemed to get more bad news. He cautiously answered as if he was afraid whoever was on the other end of it would jump out at him. Some of the uneasiness left him when he heard that it was Robert.

"Didn't ditch the phone yet, huh?"

"I will."

"OK. How are you holding up?" Robert asked.

"As well as can be expected I guess. I just want this to be over."

"It will be soon."

"How do you know, you got something?" Spencer optimistically asked.

"Maybe. I saw that you broke into Wilson Marcus' house earlier, did you find anything?"

"No. I checked his computer and went through his desk, but nothing that'd seem to help."

"Stands to reason. He's not that careless."

"You said you might have something."

"Yeah, I've got papers that specify you being the target of a hit. I pulled a lot of favors to get these so fast."

"Do they actually sign contracts for that?"

"No. There are no official records between two parties. The organization keeps their own records of all transactions though. All phone calls are recorded, e-mails saved, letters and faxes filed. They like the information handy for future reference if needed."

"When can you give it to me?"

"Tonight."

"Where?"

"I'll meet you on North Chinton Avenue. I'll be waiting at the corner in a black SUV."

"I'll be there, what time?"

"Let's make it ten. If you're not there within five minutes I'm gone."

"Understood."

"Good. One more thing, the news said that you had a woman helping you. Is that right?"

"Yes."

"Are you sure she's someone you can trust?"

"Yes. I've already given her the chance to turn me in, and she didn't take it."

"Good, just be careful, you never know."

"I will be."

"Alright, I'll see you at ten then," Robert said.

"Wait," Spencer hurriedly muttered before Robert hung up.

"What?"

"He called me."

"When?"

"At the hotel right after you did."

"What'd he say?"

"He told me why he killed Stacy, and that if I turned myself in or went to the police voluntarily he'd kill my parents."

"Doesn't surprise me. When something goes wrong on a hit it becomes a problem. You contain that problem by taking away his options. Unless you hate your parents, he's contained your options."

"Would he do it?"

"Without hesitation."

"So what do I do? I can't stay on the run, and I can't go to the police."

Robert took a few seconds before answering.

"I'd say you have three choices."

"What are they?" Spencer asked knowing he probably wouldn't like any of them.

"You could turn yourself in and present the evidence I give you along with your side of the story and take your chances."

"That'd endanger my parents and I will not do that to them."

"Then you could accept what's happened and try to set up a new life elsewhere. New name, new city, new ID's, new everything."

"I don't know if I could do that. I'd always think someone was just around the corner ready for me."

"Then there's the last option, you eliminate your problem."

"You mean kill him."

"Yes."

Spencer stammered a bit before composing himself to talk clearly.

"How could I do that? He's a professional. I'm just an accountant; I've never been violent or hurt anyone before."

"I can help with that. The next time he calls, you set up a meet with him. Say whatever you have to in order to get him there. Then I'll be there waiting for him, and I'll kill him."

"What makes you think he'll call me again?"

"To make sure he's still in the back of your mind. He wants you to worry about him so you'll make a mistake. He figures the more you worry about him, the more mistakes you'll make."

"OK."

"Alright, I'll see you later."

After hanging up the phone, Spencer looked over to Samantha. She could tell he was a little shaken by whatever Robert had told him.

"What is it?" she asked.

"I have to meet him tonight."

"Why?"

"He's got something that'll help."

Spencer spent the next few hours trying to keep himself busy so he wouldn't think about his problems as much. He tried reading, watching TV, doing a crossword puzzle, but nothing helped. No matter what he tried, his mind kept replaying the events of the prior few days. He also kept thinking about Robert. He was anxious to get the night over with. Although he felt he could trust Robert, at least as much as he could trust anyone, he still knew he needed to be cautious.

The hours passed in what seemed like minutes to him. It was 9:30. Spencer picked up his gun from the table and saw Samantha pick up the keys to the car.

"What do you think you're doing?"

"I'm going with you," she answered.

"No, not this time. I don't know what might happen out there. If something bad happens I don't want you in the middle of it."

"Which is exactly why you need me with you. If you need to get out of there in a hurry, I'll have the car ready and waiting for you."

"Samantha…" Spencer said, his voice trailing off in frustration. He knew he was wasting his breath.

"I'm not taking no for an answer. Where you go, I go."

"Alright, let's go."

As they drove to meet Robert, Spencer tried to mentally prepare himself for anything that might happen. Spencer and Samantha didn't say a word to each other on the way. She could tell he had things going through his mind. All of a sudden Spencer looked up and he saw the black

SUV that Robert said he'd be waiting in. He was almost paralyzed by the sight of the vehicle. Spencer looked down at the clock and watched it change to 10:01.

"Be careful," Samantha said, as she and Spencer looked at each other.

"I will. Keep your eyes open."

Spencer willed himself to get out of the car and quickly glanced around but saw nothing suspicious. He cautiously approached the SUV stopping at the rear of the truck. He looked in the window and saw nothing but the outline of someone sitting in the driver's seat. He made his way to the front passenger door and slowly opened it. He peeked his head in, noticing the man was leaning back in the seat but kept looking out his window. Spencer got in the SUV and turned toward the man in the driver's seat.

"Robert?"

The man didn't answer him. Spencer was getting a little more worried with the silence he was getting. Spencer didn't want to make any sudden movements that would alarm the man, but slowly reached his arm out touching the driver's shoulder. As soon as Spencer touched him he slumped over, his head hitting the steering wheel. Spencer's eyes widened not knowing exactly what to do. He looked around to see if maybe he was the next target. Spencer figured it had to be his pursuer. If he knew where Robert was, and what he was doing, then he surely must've known whom he was there to meet. But he saw nothing coming towards the truck.

Spencer pulled Robert back so he'd be leaning against the seat again. He pulled Robert's jacket open slightly and saw his blood stained shirt. Spencer pulled back a little horrified by the sight of the dead body in front of him. He glanced down at the floor and noticed a knife by Robert's feet. He reached down to pick it up but caught himself before he did. If it was the murder weapon then he wouldn't want to touch it and get his prints on it. The last thing he needed was to be accused of another murder.

Then Spencer thought of why he was there to begin with. Robert was supposed to give him some evidence that'd help clear him. Spencer opened the glove compartment and rifled through it but saw nothing that was of any interest to him. He looked down on the floor, by the seats, and even turned around to see if anything was on the back seats but again turned up nothing.

"Damn," Spencer yelled. He was frustrated at being so close to getting something valuable, but still coming out of it empty handed. He was beginning to think he'd never get out of this. Maybe it was just destiny that he wouldn't be able to work things out. He got out of the car and saw a man leaning against the wall on the corner. Spencer just stood there a few seconds waiting to see if the man would make a move. He didn't.

Moments later Spencer heard police sirens. They didn't seem to be far away. In fact, they seemed to be coming closer by the second. Spencer raced toward Samantha's car and quickly got in. Samantha speedily drove off before any police cars had gotten there.

"Did you get anything?" Samantha eagerly asked.

"No," Spencer sighed.

"Why not? What'd he say?"

"He didn't say anything. He's dead."

Samantha just shot Spencer a look of disbelief when she heard that. Spencer started talking about the scene he saw.

"He was just sitting there. I reached out and touched him and he slumped over. He was bloody then I saw a knife on the floor. I checked to see if there were any papers anywhere but there wasn't."

Samantha could tell how disappointed he was by the tone of his voice. Both Samantha and Spencer kept nervously checking to see if there were any police cars were following them, but neither saw a sign of any. They appeared to be safe for the present time.

An hour later Collins and his team had arrived at the murder scene. Their presence had been requested since someone witnessed a man matching Spencer's description leaving the truck. Collins approached the police officer that was first on the scene.

"What's the story here, officer?"

"Well, we got a call about a possible drug deal going down. We got here and found a dead body in the driver's seat. That's about it."

"Any trace of drugs?"

"Nothing. The car's totally clean."

"How was he killed?"

"Knife in the stomach. Weapon was on the floor by his feet."

"How bout this witness?"

"Standing right over there," the officer stated, pointing him in the right direction.

"Marty, you got that picture of Spencer?" Collins asked.

Stewart handed the picture of Spencer to Collins, who walked over to where the witness was standing.

"How you doing sir?" Collins asked.

"OK I guess."

"I understand you saw a man get out of that black SUV there."

"Yes, I did."

"Think you'd recognize him if you saw a picture of him?"

"I think so."

"Is this the man?" Collins asked, handing the witness Spencer's picture.

It only took the man a few seconds to answer.

"Yep, that's him."

"Thank you," Collins said while taking the picture back.

"I guess he's the one who killed that guy?" the witness assumed.

"It's possible. Did you notice how he left, whether it was by foot or car?"

"By car. He got out of the truck, then looked at me for a second. I thought he might make a move at me or something, you know? Then he heard the sirens and ran towards his car and off they went."

"They? Someone else was with him?"

"Yeah, a woman. She was driving."

"Get a good look at her?"

"No, not really. They left so fast. All I could tell is that she had blonde hair."

"Did you see anyone else in the area besides those two?"

"Nope. They were it."

"Was he carrying anything when he stepped out of the vehicle?"

"No, he wasn't carrying anything."

"How long were you standing there?"

"Just a few seconds. I got there just as he was getting out."

"Well, that should do it. Thanks for your help."

Collins then saw Stewart and Scott huddling together and approached the two of them.

"What are you knuckleheads rambling on about?" Collins remarked.

"Oh, we were just wondering how someone of your obvious higher intelligence and capabilities hasn't been able to find this guy yet. Must be slipping," Stewart sarcastically said while shaking his head.

Collins gave a half smile. He enjoyed the banter that he and Stewart often had, though he never wanted to show it too much.

"That's good. Clever, very clever."

"Did he ID Spencer?" Scott asked.

"Yes he did. The blonde woman was also with him. Have they found any prints on the vehicle or the weapon?" Collins asked.

"No prints on the weapon, it was wiped clean. Blood on the blade but that's it. They have a couple prints on the passenger side door."

Collins took a look for himself inside the vehicle. He then sat in the passenger seat and thought about how things might have gone. He stepped out of the truck and folded his arms with his hand on his chin.

"Uh oh. What are you thinking about chief?" Stewart asked.

"Like every other part of this case, this doesn't make sense either."

"Who is this guy?" Collins animatedly asked.

"What guy?"

"The dead guy. Any ID on him?"

"Oh. Yeah. He had about five different ID's on him, including a social security card, which has him as a Robert Hurst. That's what we're going by right now. We're running him right now for more info."

"Alright, everything's taken care of here, we're not going to get any more of a lead on where he's going now so I'm going back to the office."

While walking to his car, Collins heard a few reporters asking questions about the murder and whether it connected to Spencer.

"Do you have a comment on the murder?" one reporter asked.

"Uh, yeah, my comment is I have no comment."

The next day at the FBI office, Collins had met up with Stewart and Scott and started going over the details of the previous night's murder. He was hoping something would provide a lead into where Spencer was or where he might be heading next.

"Alright, let's start going over what we got. Did you get the run-down on Hurst or whatever his name is, Marty?"

"Sure do. His name is in fact Robert Hurst, though he's got a dozen aliases, half of which we saw the ID's for. He also has a sheet on him as long as all our arms put together."

"What for?" Collins eagerly asked.

"No convictions, but he was wanted for two murders in 1993 in which he was a top suspect. He's also wanted by the local, state, and federal authorities in eight states-New York, Pennsylvania, New Jersey, Maryland, Virginia, Delaware, North Carolina, and Ohio for questioning in fourteen other murders."

"Oh my. How the hell does he tie in with Spencer?"

"He's also suspected of having ties to numerous crime families and organizations."

"He was one dangerous mother."

"Was is the key word."

"Do you have anything on the victims in the murders he's wanted for?"

"Yeah, all were involved in some sort of criminal activity. Drug cases, a few who were witness in criminal investigations, I mean the list goes on and on."

"This guy was a hitman," Collins stated in shock.

"A numero uno hitman. He wasn't just some run-of-the-mill slob who was pulled off the streets. He was the preferred weapon of choice. The guy knew how to kill without being seen, he could blend in, escape, change identities, appearances, all before anybody knew what they were looking for."

"Which brings up the burning question of the day, gentlemen. How does a guy like this wind up with Ray Spencer?"

Nobody had any answers. It was a stunning development. Though there were still many questions to be answered about the case, they thought they had a general idea of what had happened and was going on. But now they seemed to have more questions than before.

"Maybe Hurst killed the girl, then Spencer killed him," Scott offered.

"No, this guy was a major player; he doesn't get involved in boyfriend-girlfriend disputes."

"Maybe Spencer was finally looking to leave town. Hurst had a million identities, knows how to blend in, etc. Spencer could've been looking to him to start a new life," Stewart explained.

"So why kill him? Beyond that, how does Spencer even get in touch with this guy? Spencer hasn't so much as a parking ticket from high school, but he knows where to find and how to get in touch with a hitman? Why does that not jive?"

Stewart didn't have an answer for that one and just scratched his head, sighing in frustration.

"And how does Robert Hurst, probably one of the best hitmen on the East Coast let himself be killed by a guy like Ray Spencer, who has no previous violent history before this past week?"

"What was bothering you last night at the scene?" Stewart asked. "You were looking at that truck like something wasn't adding up."

"Well, the knife was wiped clean right? No prints or smudges or anything."

"Yeah."

"But there are prints on the door. Nathan, did you check to see if those prints match the ones we have on Spencer?"

"Yeah, I did. They match."

"See, that's the problem."

"I'm not following," Stewart confessed.

"Let's say Spencer kills him OK? He's consciously aware of the fact that his prints might get on the knife, and he doesn't want that, so what's he do?"

"He wears gloves," Stewart answered.

"So how do the prints get on the door?"

"So he didn't wear gloves, he used something to wipe the handle."

"So he's consciously aware enough in his mind to wipe the handle of the knife, but he forgets to do the same with the door?"

"You're right, it doesn't make sense."

"Know what I think?"

"What's that?"

"I think we're trying to force this."

"In what way?"

"We've got too many things that aren't making sense, and we're trying to tie them all together to indicate Ray Spencer's doing everything. Maybe we're ignoring other possibilities."

"Like what? We've got no other motives, or suspects. He's the only person who keeps popping up," Stewart said.

"Let's forget about everything else that's happened so far and just concentrate on this murder here. What connection would Hurst and Spencer have?"

"Well, considering Hurst's history I'd say that Spencer hired him to kill someone."

"OK, now let's figure out why. It doesn't involve drugs since Spencer's not a user. What else would attract a hit on someone considering Spencer's profession?"

"Scandal," Stewart excitedly answered. "A scandal could bring a company to its knees. There's been a lot of that lately with Enron and Arthur Andersen. Maybe Hartwell Enterprises has a problem with its accounting practices too."

Collins just nodded his head in agreement thinking that Stewart may just have hit on the break they were looking for.

"Nathan, go check and see if there's been any complaints, lawsuits, questions, irregularities, anything at all filed against Hartwell Enterprises in the last year."

"We could be on to something," Stewart said.

"Maybe. We don't have anything concrete yet though, it's just another possibility."

"What next?"

"We wait to see what Nate turns up. Then we go have another chat with our friend Wilson Marcus."

7

Spencer had been stewing around all morning trying to think of another way out of his predicament. He figured that the only place left that he could go was the Hartwell Enterprises building. He was planning on going the previous night before Robert contacted him about meeting so he put it off. Now he had no other place to go though. There was no other option.

While he was debating about when the best time to go would be, he remembered what Robert told him about sticking to moving at night so as not to be seen and blend into the environment. Then he could search the building knowing he had some time and nobody would surprise him. But there was a part of him who wanted to charge right into that building and confront Wilson Marcus. Maybe he could put a scare into him and make him divulge some information that he could use.

Spencer noticed Samantha sitting in the living room watching TV. Her eyes seemed to be glued to the screen. He was almost afraid to ask what she was watching. He had a feeling his latest escapade had just been added to his string of headline news appearances.

"What are you watching?"

"Just about last night."

"Thought so. What are they saying?"

"They're just assuming that you did it."

"Of course they are," he dejectedly said.

"Hey, be positive. We'll find a way to get out of this."

After realizing that her words weren't having much effect on Spencer, Samantha walked over to him and gave him a hug. She pulled away from him just enough to put her hands on the sides of his face while she looked in his eyes.

"We'll find a way."

Spencer couldn't help but nod his head and smile. It was a simple gesture but she made him feel a little bit better.

"We're gonna have to go to the Hartwell Enterprises building," Spencer told her.

"When?"

"Well I figure we can either go today and I can confront Wilson Marcus or we can go later tonight when nobody's there."

"When do you think is best? It's dangerous to go during the day when you can be easily spotted."

"I know. I guess it'd be better to go later tonight, huh?"

"Yeah, I think so. Besides, you can always go back to Marcus' house if you want to talk to him."

"You're right. We'll wait till later."

"Who do you think killed Robert last night?" Samantha asked.

Spencer hesitated before answering as if to think about it first, though he was certain as to who it was that killed him.

"It could only be one person. It had to be him," Spencer said, referring to the man who attacked him at his house.

"But how did he know?"

"I don't know. Maybe he found out where Robert was and followed him there."

"What if he followed us too? Maybe he knows where we're at too? Or if it was him then why didn't he wait and attack you there too?" Samantha asked nervously.

"I think if he knew where we were we'd know it by now. Maybe he didn't know who Robert was there to meet. Or maybe he knew who but didn't know when and didn't want to keep waiting around without knowing."

"You're probably right."

"Besides, he can afford to wait. He doesn't need to be in a hurry."

The two of them then sat beside each other on the couch watching more of the news. Spencer turned his head to look at Samantha and he started thinking of everything she had done for him. If it wasn't for her help he was sure he'd probably be in jail by now.

"Thank you," he blurted out.

She looked back at him and smiled wondering what she was being thanked for.

"What are you thanking me for?"

"For trusting me and for helping me. I don't think anybody else would do what you've done for me."

"You're welcome. I don't know though, I'm sure a lot of people would do what I've done if they were in the same situation."

"I don't know about that. I don't think most people are very trusting. Not that I'd blame them."

"You were honest with me and told me the truth about everything that happened, so why wouldn't I trust you?"

"What made you believe me? I could've been lying."

"Because there was no reason for you to lie to me. You tried too hard to convince me that you were innocent. I don't think someone who was guilty would've tried so hard. If you were guilty I think I probably would've been dead on the highway when I picked you up. You'd have had nothing to lose by killing me."

"You're very perceptive."

"I know," she said with a smile.

Stewart ran into Scott in the hallway of the FBI building, as he was about to report his findings of Hartwell Enterprises.

"Did you get anything?" Stewart asked.

"Oh, Bill's gonna like what I got."

"Maybe we're actually starting to make some headway on this case."

"I think we're getting close," Scott replied.

Collins was on the phone when the two agents walked into his office. He motioned them to sit down while he finished up talking.

"Yeah…yeah…yeah," Collins hurriedly said as he hung up the phone. "Alright what do you guys got? Tell me it's good news."

"The lowdown on Hartwell Enterprises is this; they've had several complaints in the past year," Scott informed them.

"What kind of complaints?" Collins asked.

"Angry shareholder complaints. Seems that some of the shareholders aren't exactly too happy with the current management team."

"Why is that?"

"There's a perception that management is more focused on making themselves money rather than taking care of their shareholders."

"This is getting good, keep going," Collins said with a laugh.

"I also called a few people this morning to check on Wilson Marcus."

"Hit me with the rest of it Nate, throw me that strikeout pitch," Collins said, starting to get animated.

"The general consensus is that he's a very ruthless, aggressive person."

"You mean he's not a boy scout too?" Collins sarcastically asked.

"Hardly. I asked if they'd heard anything about whether there was anything funny going on in the company, and while nobody said they knew of anything, they all said that they wouldn't be shocked if he put money in categories that they shouldn't be in."

"How bout a violent streak?" Stewart asked.

"Apparently under those expensive suits lies a very bad temper. The word is that he's not a man you want to cross."

"The question is did Ray Spencer cross him?"

"We seem to be getting sidetracked here chief," Stewart said.

"How's that?"

"We started this out as a murder case involving Ray Spencer, and now we're looking into cooked books and Wilson Marcus and who knows else what."

"What we're looking for is motive. Did Ray Spencer kill his girlfriend? If he did, then why? Cooked books could be the answer. Maybe they fought about whether to turn evidence. If Spencer didn't kill her, then someone else did. If someone else did, then why? Again, cooked books could be the answer. And Wilson Marcus seems like a good fit to either possibility."

"So you're not sure Ray Spencer killed his girlfriend or Robert Hurst?" Stewart asked.

"I'm not saying he didn't do it, Marty. But we still have no concrete evidence that he killed either. We still don't have the murder weapon from Hill. The knife on Hurst has no prints on it. Right now all we have are theories and assumptions. What we need right now are some cold hard facts."

Collins then thought of something and started looking through the papers on his desk. Stewart and Scott could tell that he was on to something. Collins then seemed to come across what he was looking for and pulled it out of the folder.

"What're you looking for?" Stewart asked.

"Just looking to see what possessions were found in his home and office."

"What for?" Stewart wondered.

"Because I don't recall seeing anything mentioned about a briefcase and it's not listed on here."

"So what?"

"So he works for a large corporation, right?"

"Yeah."

"Don't you think he occasionally might take things home to work on?"

"Probably."

"How do you think he'll carry that stuff?"

"In a briefcase," Stewart said.

"Which brings up one more question. Did he have one and where'd it go?"

"One thing's for sure…it didn't just walk out on its own," Stewart stated.

"See, that's witty. You're learning. A few more of those and you'll be right up there with me. Not quite as good as the cookie crumbling but it's close," Collins shot back.

"Oh great, now I'm in real trouble. I'm starting to think like you."

"What say we take a little visit over to Wilson Marcus and get some answers?"

The agents then left for the Hartwell Enterprises building and upon arriving noticed Wilson Marcus' car. They walked over to it and looked inside through the windows though they weren't really looking for anything in particular.

"Nice car," Collins stated.

"I'd say so," Stewart responded.

"How much you think it runs?"

"Sixty to seventy thousand."

"Think maybe I can afford a car like that some day?" Collins asked.

"Not unless you change professions."

"How much does Marcus make?"

"A few hundred thousand."

"I should've become an accountant."

"Then you never would've met me. Think of how much more boring your life would be."

"Forget the money, not meeting you is reason enough right there."

"You know you love me."

They then entered the building and took the elevator up to Wilson Marcus' office. Once they hit the floor his office was on they told his secretary to inform him that they were there. Moments later Marcus emerged from his office and greeted the agents.

"Agent Collins, Agent Stewart, how can I be of assistance today?"

"I think it'd be best if we talked inside your office," Collins informed him.

Marcus let them in and told his secretary that he was not to be disturbed while the agents were there. Marcus sat behind his desk wondering what they wanted him for. He was beginning to feel like they were suspecting him of something.

"Please be seated gentlemen. I must admit that I'm a little surprised to see you. What brings you down here today?"

"You bring us down here, Mr. Marcus," Collins stated matter-of-factly.

"I'm afraid you have me at a loss Agent Collins," Marcus said clasping his hands together on the desk.

"First thing I wanna know is did Ray Spencer have a briefcase?"

"Yes, we all have them."

"What color was it?"

"Brown I believe. Is that why you're here? About a briefcase?"

"Well it seems to be missing. It wasn't found in his office, house, or car. So that brings us to a natural assumption that there's something in it that's of value to him. Any ideas as to what?"

Marcus didn't know how to respond and just threw his hands up slightly suggesting that he had no answer.

"Have you or any of your people noticed anything missing in the last few days, something he may have taken with him?"

"I've had nobody mention anything to me and I, myself, haven't noticed anything."

There was silence between the three men for a few seconds leading Marcus to believe they were through with him. He stood up, ready to lead them out of his office.

"Well, if that'll be all gentlemen," Marcus said hopefully.

"There's a few more things we'd like to talk to you about if you have the time," Collins said.

"Well, it's a big company and I have many things to do, but I think I can spare a few more minutes," he said looking at his watch before sitting back down.

"I was looking at your car outside before we came in. Impressive."

"Thank you. I like the best of everything."

"I had a feeling you did. What would happen if you could no longer afford the best of everything?"

"I'm not quite sure I catch your meaning."

"What would happen if Hartwell Enterprises had some difficulties financially? That'd put you in a pretty tough spot would it not?"

"We're in no financial troubles I assure you."

"As the books are stated now you're not," Collins said bluntly.

"What is it that you're implying?"

"We've done some checking about the state of the company recently and it seems there are some who are not too high on the management team."

"There will always be those who disagree with those in power positions," Marcus said with a shrug.

"There's been several complaints over the past year about how the company operates financially."

"I'm aware of those."

"Was Ray Spencer aware of those?" Stewart asked.

"Everyone is aware of any complaint levied against the company."

"You have a reputation of being a very ruthless, aggressive type of person," Collins said.

Marcus smiled at the assertion.

"I think anybody who gets to the position I have, gets there by being very ruthless and very aggressive. That's not a unique quality."

"No, I guess not. Well, I guess I've pretty much danced around this long enough so I'll just come right out and say it. There are some who wouldn't be at all surprised to learn that Hartwell Enterprises isn't doing as well as it would seem due to some unnecessary bookkeeping adjustments, if you know what I mean."

"Yes, I do know what you mean. I'd be careful with my assumptions and accusations if I were you, Agent Collins, lawsuits can be a very ugly, messy, and unpleasant process. We have been audited and nothing has been found to be unusual."

"Enron was audited too. Didn't seem to stop them. Hell, they didn't even pay their taxes for a few years," Collins said.

"Is there anything else I can do for you gentlemen? I really do have to be going now."

"I think that'll cover it for today. We'll be in touch again."

"I'm sure you will. Only the next time you have questions, make sure you have some evidence that corroborates what you ask. Some people may take what you say the wrong way and perceive it as a personal attack or an accusation. The next time my attorney will be present to make sure the questioning doesn't get out of hand, shall we say?"

"Let me tell you something, Mr. Marcus, I don't care if you bring your attorney, your hairdresser, your masseuse, or the president of the Dogcatchers of America Association. Believe me, the questions won't change. Stick in the area, Mr. Marcus, you'll be seeing us again," Collins said as he walked out of the office.

"Looks like we struck a nerve," Stewart noted.

"Oh yeah. Nobody mentions their attorney being present unless they're worried or have something to hide. He's definitely got the jitters."

8

As the night progressed Spencer started to become noticeably more nervous. Samantha could tell how anxious he was by his mannerisms. He was either pacing in the living room or kitchen, or he was tapping his foot or fingers while he was sitting down. Samantha started talking to him but he was so deep in thought that he didn't hear a word she was saying. She finally walked over to him and stood in front of him so he'd be sure to hear what she said.

"Ray?"

He finally snapped out of his trance and was aware of Samantha's presence.

"What?" he asked, knowing she said something that he missed.

"What are you thinking about?"

"Nothing new."

"Tell me what you're thinking."

"This has to end soon. With each day they're getting closer to finding me, I can feel it. And with Robert gone, I've got no one else to help me."

"What about me?"

"I didn't mean it like that. I meant he's the only person on the outside that can actually get evidence to clear me. You've done more than I can ever repay."

"So what now, General?" she said with a smile.

"Let's go take a ride."

"To the office?

Spencer answered with a simple nod of his head. They left the house shortly afterward to go to the Hartwell Enterprises building. As they approached the building, Spencer noticed a car across the street. Although he saw nothing unusual about the car, he got an uneasy feeling about it. He told Samantha to keep driving. Spencer told her to drive around to the back of the building where there was another less noticeable entrance.

As Samantha parked the car Spencer glanced around for anything that might seem troubling. Everything seemed to be OK. Before getting out of the car, Spencer told Samantha to stay out of sight and that he'd be back in a few minutes. He knew he wouldn't have long to look around. There was a silent alarm that would go off as soon as he broke in.

Spencer brought a bat with him to break the glass in the door. He broke the glass with the knob of the bat and let himself in. He rushed to the elevator to get to Wilson Marcus' office on the tenth floor. Once he reached the tenth floor, he quickly ran over to Marcus' office, but found that his door was locked. He kicked the door a couple of times till it swung open. He swiftly moved around the desk opening the drawers. Looking through the drawers, he found nothing that would indicate any type of illegal activities.

Although he had to search quickly he was trying not to go so fast that he might miss something. He went over to a file cabinet and started rifling through the folders that were in it. He found some of the company's financial statements, but that in itself wouldn't prove anything. He would need all the accounts, ledgers, and journals and go through them to prove that the statements are false or misleading. Even if he did get them though, that'd still only prove that the company was misstating its numbers. It really wouldn't do much to prove that he didn't kill his girlfriend or Robert.

A few minutes had passed and Spencer figured that his time was up. If he spent any more time there he was risking getting caught. He ran out of the office and into the elevator sweating every second he was in it. He nervously waited as the elevator passed each floor on the way down. Anxiously, Spencer kept looking at the numbers as he counted down, the numbers declining in what seemed to be slow motion. He got a bad feeling that when the doors opened the police would be there waiting for him with open arms.

Spencer looked a little wild-eyed as the doors opened hoping what he imagined would not turn out to be a reality. He stepped out and looked almost surprised that he was still alone. He then let out a sigh of relief. He bolted out the door and into Samantha's car as she drove away.

Samantha noticed that Spencer wasn't carrying anything out with him and assumed that he didn't find anything worthwhile.

"Didn't find anything?"

"Not really. There really wasn't enough time, but I didn't want to stay in there too long though. It was pretty much like looking for a needle in a haystack. But it was worth a shot I guess."

"Where did you look?"

"Just went through his desk drawers and a file cabinet. I was just looking for something to jump out at me. I didn't really have enough time to look through every single thing. The police are probably getting there about now to respond to the silent alarm that went off."

"Do you think maybe we can go back later? Maybe we can find a way to stay for a longer period," Samantha proposed.

"I don't think so. I imagine they'll be on the lookout for something else now. I don't see how we could try this again unless…" Spencer said, not finishing what he was thinking.

"What?"

"Just an idea, but I think it might be too dangerous. Very risky."

"What is it?"

"We could come back during the daytime. Nobody would be expecting it. But once we're seen it'd put us in a vulnerable position."

"Do we have any other choices?" Samantha asked in a tone clearly indicating that she was in favor of it.

"Not really," Spencer dejectedly answered as he stared out the window. "I don't know what else to do. I can't go to the police or my parents are dead. Even if I did, I don't have any evidence to support anything. But if I don't get something soon, eventually this guy trailing me is going to find me. It seems like there's no way out. Maybe I should just let the police find me and take whatever's handed out."

"You can't do that."

"Why not?"

"Because you're innocent. Don't stop fighting."

They arrived back at Samantha's house and tried thinking of ideas to clear Spencer. Samantha thought of sending a letter to the police explaining everything, but Spencer thought it'd be a waste of time. After all, how would they know whether they would believe his story without actually talking to him. If they didn't believe it, that'd be just like giving himself up. Or they could think he's just some nutball trying to throw them off his trail. The only other thing either of them could think of was to talk to Marcus himself. He might do or say something that would help Spencer's case.

The FBI arrived at Hartwell Enterprises in the morning once they received word of the break-in. They were sure Spencer had something to do with it. Collins and Stewart first wandered over to the door where he broke in, analyzing it for a few minutes. They then went up to Marcus' office. They talked to a few of the detectives that were already there to determine what happened. Collins asked if they found any fingerprints. One agent told him they had, but they were all over the place and no telling when they had gotten there.

"I don't think we really need any prints to know who this was," Collins stated.

A few minutes later, Wilson Marcus entered the room.

"How are you doing today, gentlemen?" Marcus asked.

"Better than you are I'd imagine," Collins countered.

"I assure you I'm quite fine."

"Nerves of steel, huh?"

"I have nothing to be nervous of."

"Still don't think he's after you, huh?"

"If he was I would assume he'd of made some type of contact with me by now."

"So you don't have any security guards in a big company like this?"

"We've never needed any until now. We do have a few security cameras though."

"Could we see them?"

Marcus called one of his employees to bring the tapes of the previous evening up to his office.

"So let me ask you a question. Where do you think Spencer's headed now?"

"I haven't the slightest idea," Marcus replied.

"He's been to your house, he's been to your office, where else do you go?"

Marcus just looked out his window without replying.

"So what was he after today?" Collins asked.

"I still don't know."

"You wouldn't be surprised then if I said I didn't believe that."

"Not in the least."

An employee brought in a couple tapes and placed them on Marcus' desk. Stewart put the tapes in the tape player and started to fast-forward through them. After a few minutes he slowed it down and they all watched as Spencer broke into the office. They had footage of him in the hallway, when he first broke into the building and outside the building.

"Slow it down a little, Marty," Collins told him.

Stewart slowed down the footage of Spencer running from the building. They watched as he got into a black car that drove away.

"Do I see what I think I do?" Collins asked to nobody in particular.

"Depends," Stewart answered.

"Do you see that license plate?"

Stewart squinted his eyes to make it out but it was too far away and too blurry.

"Mr. Marcus, we'll have to confiscate this tape to analyze it," Collins said.

"Absolutely."

They took it back to the FBI building to get the tape looked at, but they were only able to get a partial plate number. The car was turning so they could only get the last four digits, but they also were able to determine the make and model of the car from the tape. Collins gave the task of tracking down the info to Scott. He came back a few hours later with a couple possible targets.

"Whatcha got, Nate?" Collins asked.

"I've got three names that have those digits on their plates and drive a black Chevy."

"And they are?"

"Dorothy White, no criminal record. Jim Bruncton, a few traffic violations. Samantha Hopkins, no criminal record."

"Well it's gotta be one of them. None of them have reported their car stolen, correct?"

"Nope."

"Well, let's go ask some questions."

They went to White's house first. She lived in a pretty nice neighborhood where the houses were all well kept, mostly an upper middle class suburb. They knocked on the door anxiously waiting for it to open. An older woman answered as the agents looked at each other.

"Can I help you?" she asked.

"We're looking for a Dorothy White," Stewart informed her.

"That's me."

She was short, had brown hair with a little gray in it, and looked to be in her 60's. Collins took out his credentials to show her they were agents.

"I don't suppose you've been to Hartwell Enterprises lately, have you?" Collins asked, not expecting a favorable response.

"Where's that?"

"I thought not. You haven't loaned your car out to anyone recently have you?"

"Oh no, I don't let anybody drive my car."

"Do you have any female family members or friends who have blonde hair?"

"Let me see…yes, I do. All my friends are going gray like me, but I do have a niece who has blonde hair, she's very pretty."

"Where could we find her?"

"Oh she lives in Texas. Would you like me to get her address for you?"

"No, that's alright. Well thank you for your time," Stewart told her.

They then drove to the house of Bruncton, also in one of the nicer neighborhoods. Jim Bruncton answered the door. They let him know that they were investigating the Spencer case.

"I heard about him. What can I do?" Bruncton asked.

"Well, your car matches a car he was spotted in last night including the last four digits of your license plate," Stewart informed him.

"My car hasn't been out of the driveway for two days."

"Does anyone else in your family have access to the keys, a daughter perhaps?"

"She's only 11."

"Could we see your wife please?"

Bruncton nervously returned a minute later with his wife. She was in her 40's and had brown curly hair.

"Appreciate your cooperation," Collins abruptly said before the men left.

On the way to Samantha's house, the agents were discussing the case.

"I sure hope this woman has blonde hair," Collins stated.

"I hate to ask this but what if she don't?" Stewart asked.

"Then I guess we go to Plan B."

"Which is what?"

"Damned if I know. I'm getting tired of thinking about this case."

Upon walking up the path to Samantha's house they were looking around.

"Nice house," Collins said.

"Yeah. Not too big, not too small, nice size."

They knocked on the door but nobody answered. The car was in the driveway so they figured somebody was home. They knocked on the door again waiting for an answer. Finally, a few minutes later, the door opened.

"Hi, are you Samantha?" Collins asked her, his eyes almost bulging out noticing her blonde hair.

"Yes, who are you?"

"I'm Agent Collins, this is Agent Stewart."

"How can I help you?"

"We're investigating a man named Ray Spencer, know him?"

"He's the one on the news, right?"

"That's him."

"I only know what I've seen on the news."

"So you don't know him?"

"No, why would I?"

"Well, he's been seen in a black car with a license plate that matches yours."

"I wouldn't let someone like that in my car."

"Do you have a boyfriend, Ms. Hopkins?"

"No, I live alone."

"Surprising. A beautiful woman like you, I'd expect you to have a boyfriend."

"I'm very picky."

"Mind if we take a look around inside?"

"Umm...I guess not."

The agents stepped inside the house and Collins immediately noticed a pillow on the couch.

"Somebody sleeping over?" he asked.

"That was me. I was taking a nap when you knocked. That's why it took me a few minutes to answer."

They looked through the entire house. They checked the bedrooms, bathroom, under the bed, inside closets, behind furniture.

"What exactly are you looking for?" Samantha asked, getting a little nervous. Spencer had ducked out the back door when the agents started knocking, but she didn't know exactly where he was.

"Ray Spencer," Collins answered.

"I told you I don't know him."

"Oh, I forgot to mention that he was seen with a blonde haired woman. That matches you."

"There's a lot of blondes out there."

"Not with your license plate."

They continued checking the house for any other signs that Spencer was or had been there. They looked out the back window but nothing seemed out of the ordinary. They began leaving after determining that he wasn't there at the moment.

"So you don't know where he's at?"

"I've never met him."

They didn't believe her. They left after leaving a card for her to contact them if she should happen to know where he was. The agents got into their car and drove down the street before turning around and parking along a curb, waiting to see some type of sign that Spencer was there.

"You think he's in there?" Stewart asked.

"Well we didn't turn him up did we?"

"No, but you think he's staying there?"

"It wouldn't surprise me. I don't know who this girl is, but I imagine she's fallen for him so she may lead us to him."

"If she knows where he's at."

"She's been spotted at two different places with him. I'm sure she knows where he is. Call Nate and get another car out here."

Stewart called Scott to meet them out there and stake out the other end of the street.

9

Spencer walked back into the house through the back door. Samantha was a little started, not fully expecting to see him again so soon. She figured he might have taken off.

"Who were those people?" he asked with a worried tone.

"FBI agents."

"They know I'm here.

"No they don't."

"They know about you."

"How could they? Wait, he said something about my license plate."

"Somebody probably got a look at it and called it in or something."

"What do we do now?"

"We can't stay here, that's for sure."

"They didn't find anything in here that would make them think you're staying here."

"Yeah, but they're probably sitting in a car down the street waiting for my face to pop up. Even if they don't think I'm here they may think I'll be here eventually. We gotta go."

"To where?"

"I don't know. We can't use your car either, they'll follow."

"What if I drive somewhere and lead them away," she offered.

"That might work."

A sense of sadness fell over her as she grabbed her keys. She thought it might be the last she'd see of him.

"Will I ever see you again?" she asked.

"I don't know," he said with a sigh, his eyes looking towards the floor.

She walked up to him and gave him a kiss on the cheek.

"Good luck," she said.

"Thank you for everything," he told her, his eyes tearing up.

She walked towards the door, giving him one last look before leaving. She started driving and immediately noticed a car following. She knew it must've been the agents that had just visited her. Spencer had gotten an idea and called for a cab to meet him a few streets over. Before leaving, he started rifling through some of Samantha's living room drawers. Suddenly he stopped, finding what he was looking for, and started talking to make sure it worked. He rewound the machine and hit play, instantly hearing what he'd just said. He slipped the recorder into his pocket and fled through the back door.

He looked around and hopped the back fence, cutting through the neighbor's yard. He continued slicing through the yards of a few more houses before meeting up with his cab. He figured Samantha must've drawn the agents away otherwise they would've nabbed him by now. He gave the cab driver the address and started to play out in his mind how he wanted the events to unfold. The driver let him out in front of the house and Spencer ran up to the front door. He looked around to see if there was a way he could get in without it being obvious, but he did not see it. He noticed a rather large clump of bushes just off the pathway and took cover behind it.

He was starting to get antsy just waiting there, but after a few hours he heard a car pull into the driveway. He heard the car door slam shut and the sound of someone walking closer towards him. As the man unlocked the front door and started to close the door, Spencer jumped out from behind the bushes, lunging towards the door much to the man's surprise. He tried to close the door before Spencer got there but Spencer bulled his way in without much resistance.

"Surprised to see me, Wilson?" Spencer asked.

"Something I can help you with Ray?" Marcus asked back.

"Yeah, you can make this all go away."

"Make what go away?"

"You know what! The murders, the running, the hiding, I want my life back!"

"Ray, you have to come to grips with yourself. Turn yourself in, I'll get you a good lawyer."

Spencer gave in to his anger, reached back, and punched Marcus, sending him stumbling toward the wall. Spencer grabbed the back of Marcus' head and slammed it into the wall several times. Marcus slumped down to the floor, his forehead starting to bleed. Marcus started crawling into another room trying to get away from Spencer, who was following him.

"You've got nowhere to go, Wilson," Spencer said angrily.

Marcus continued crawling slowly, until he reached a chair that he managed to pull himself onto.

"You're making a mistake, Ray."

"I don't think so," Spencer countered, knocking him off the chair with another punch.

Marcus pulled himself back up onto the chair again.

"What do you want from me?"

"I want the truth," Spencer replied.

"About what?"

"About why this is happening!"

"You already know why this is happening," Marcus wearily said.

"I swear that if you don't start talking you'll never see another day on this planet," Spencer said as he pulled his gun, pointing it at Marcus.

"If you shoot me you'll go to jail for sure."

"So what? If I'm going there for murders I didn't commit, I might as well go there for one I did. I'll only tell you one more time...start talking."

"What do you want me to say?"

"How long did you know I was checking into the books?"

"About a month."

"How'd you find out?"

"Stacey called me one day and told me what you were doing."

"So why'd you have her killed?"

"She kept asking for more money. She became a nuisance that wasn't necessary. Tough to believe that someone you love sold you out, huh? But money talks, and love takes a back seat when it comes to money."

"Why go through all this?"

"Because you would've taken the company down. I couldn't let that happen."

"So who came up with this elaborate plan to make me the fall guy?"

"I did. I didn't count on you being this elusive though. I underestimated you."

"Who's the hitman?"

"I have no idea what his real name is."

"Where can I find him?"

"He'll find you."

"How do you contact him?"

"He contacts me."

"I wanna meet with him."

"Your funeral," Marcus said with a shrug.

"How often does he contact you?"

"Every couple days."

"Is he due?"

"Probably."

"Tell him it ends now."

"Just get out of the country Ray; it's the only chance you've got. If you leave, I'll call him off. Why continue to put yourself through this agony?"

"Because I want to see you see dead."

"Won't happen."

"We'll see. Where's my briefcase?"

"I don't have it."

"So who does?"

"It's probably burned by now. You'll never get it back. You'll never be able to prove anything," Marcus said, finally unleashing an evil grin.

"I think I'd be OK with that as long as I take you down with me."

"That won't happen. All the paper trails have been erased. You've got nothing going for you."

"That's all I wanted to know. I'll call in two days to set up a meeting with your boy. Try following me, and I'll unload every bullet I've got."

"Wouldn't dream of it."

Spencer slowly backed away before running out the front door. He walked a few blocks to a supermarket and grabbed another cab. He asked the driver to take him to his parent's house. He was hesitant to put them in any danger, but he didn't know where else to go or who else to turn to. He was running out of options. He told the driver to stop a street over just in case someone was watching the house. He wound up going through the backyard and climbed through an open patio window. He started knocking on the back door to get his parents attention. They looked out the kitchen window and saw Spencer, rushing out to the patio giving him a hug.

Samantha had led the agents to a supermarket, a bookstore, and a couple of retail stores. She was just driving to kill some time.

"Where is she heading now?" Stewart asked.

"She knows we're on her," Collins said.

"You think this is a wild goose chase?"

"Most likely."

"But where's Spencer? He's not at the house; she must be going to meet him."

"We'll find out soon enough."

Samantha had stopped at a local shopping mall. She just started going in and out of stores, browsing the time away. She saw that they were still following and figured that Spencer had been able to get away otherwise they would've stopped following by now. Although she was glad she was still able to help him out in some way, she wished she were still with him. She didn't like not knowing what was happening with him. She bought a soda and just took a seat in the food court. She kept glancing down at her watch and staring out into the distance, thinking about Spencer. Collins and Stewart waited to the side where she couldn't see them for about an hour before they finally figured that Spencer wasn't going to show up. Instead of leaving they decided to walk up to Samantha's table.

"Mind if we sit down, Ms. Hopkins," Collins politely asked.

She was a little surprised that they made themselves known, but she wasn't unhappy to talk to them. Maybe they had some news on Spencer.

"Sure," she replied.

"You've been all over the place since we talked at your house," Collins stated.

"I had a lot of errands."

"I don't think so. You knew we were following you and wanted to lead us away from Spencer."

Samantha just shrugged and looked away.

"Ms. Hopkins, we have every reason to believe you've been with Spencer for the last few days and can arrest you as an accomplice."

"I told you, I don't know him."

"We think you do."

"I haven't done anything wrong."

Collins was trying to handle the situation delicately and not get animated or get Samantha upset. He figured the best option to get any information from her was for everyone to keep calm and to gain his trust.

"Ms. Hopkins, I don't want to bully you, I don't want to arrest you, I don't want to harass you, but I need to find Ray Spencer and get him off the streets."

"What if he didn't do what you think he did?"

"If he didn't, then why is he on the run?"

"Maybe cause he has no choice."

"There's always a choice."

"Not always."

"Do you know where he's heading?"

"I don't know," she said softly.

Collins sat there silently for a few moments looking at Samantha with his fingers rubbing his jaw, as if he was trying to determine whether he believed what she was saying.

"How bout we play some hypotheticals?" Collins asked.

Samantha looked at him somewhat curiously.

"If you did know Ray Spencer, do you think he would've contacted his parents by now?"

"Probably not. He wouldn't put them in danger."

"Why would this blonde girl he's been seen with keep hanging around him?"

"Hypothetically?" she asked.

"Of course."

"She believes in his innocence."

"Why would she do that?"

"Because he gave her opportunities to turn him in."

"So why would a perceived killer stay in the area and risk being caught going back to his boss' house and where he used to work?"

"Probably to try and prove that he's innocent."

"Is he succeeding?"

"Probably not."

"Would she still know where he is?"

"Not anymore."

10

Spencer and his parents started catching up on all that had happened. He told them every detail without leaving even the smallest thing out. They believed everything he told them and didn't have a single doubt in their minds about anything. They listened to the tape Spencer just recorded of his conversation with Marcus.

"You've got to let the FBI hear this tape, son."

"I don't know if it's enough."

"It's a start. It's more than you had yesterday."

"I don't know what else I can really do. I've run out of options."

"Well, we'll figure that out later. But you'll stay here the rest of the night."

"I don't think I can, every minute I stay here I put both of you in danger."

"That's the chance we'll take."

Spencer took a nap on the couch for about two hours until he was awoken by a knock on the door. He ran over to the window, peering through the curtains to see if he could make out the visitor. He couldn't see a car in the driveway or the street. His dad went to the door with his son following behind him. Spencer clung to the wall, the door giving him cover as his father opened it.

"Can I help you?" the elder Spencer asked.

"Is Ray here?" the woman asked.

"Who are you?"

"My name's Samantha. I've been helping Ray the last few days."

"I guess I should say thank you, then, for helping my son."

"No thanks are necessary. I just don't know where he's at now. We got separated yesterday, and I'm trying to find him," she said, biting her lip out of nervousness.

"Sounds like you're fond of him."

"Wouldn't be doing this if I wasn't."

He glanced over to his son, who nodded to him, giving him the signal to let her in.

"Is he here?" she asked with a touch of excitement in her voice.

"Come on in."

She slowly entered the house and turned slightly, seeing Spencer, and eagerly hugged him.

"What are you doing here?" Spencer asked.

"Looking for you. I didn't know where else to look."

"What happened earlier?"

"I led them a few places and then they finally asked me more questions."

"How do you know you weren't followed here?"

"Don't worry, I took a cab here."

"Where's your car?"

"Well after they talked to me again, I figured they'd still follow me so I led them to the airport. Before I was in real estate I was a flight attendant. I know that place like the back of my hand," she said with a smile.

"Well, I can't say it's not good to see you. What else did they talk to you about?"

"Since I wasn't really saying much, they started asking hypothetical questions about you. So I gave hypothetical answers basically trying to let them know you were innocent."

"What'd they say?"

"I don't think they really believed it."

"Not surprising. Well, while you were gone I went to Marcus' house and tape recorded our conversation."

"Does he say anything?"

"I'll let you listen."

Spencer then played the recording for Samantha to get her take on it. After it was done, Spencer, his parents, and Samantha sat down and discussed some options.

"I think we should take the tape to the FBI," Samantha said.

"I agree," Spencer's father said.

Spencer looked to his mother to get her thoughts.

"Right now, I think it's the only way," she said.

"We'll make a copy so we have one just in case, but even if it just gets their minds thinking in a different direction, it'd be worth it. I don't see a negative," his father told him.

"So how do we take it to them?" Spencer asked the group.

"I'll take it and ask that it's given to Collins," Samantha said.

"That's the way to go," his father stated.

Spencer agreed that there really wasn't any downside to taking a chance with it. The worst that could happen is that they didn't believe him. It really wouldn't have changed anything anyway. The best-case scenario was that they did believe the tape and he'd be cleared.

Just as Samantha was about to leave, the phone started ringing. Spencer's dad picked it up and was a little stunned when someone asked for Ray. Nobody should've known he was there.

"Who is this?" he asked.

"Wilson Marcus, is Ray there?"

"Wilson Marcus, you were Ray's boss weren't you?"

"Yes."

As soon as Spencer heard that it was Marcus he sprinted to the phone and grabbed it from his father's hand.

"I'm surprised to hear from you already," Spencer said.

"I've never been one to waste time, Ray, you know that."

"How'd you know I was here?"

"I didn't. I just took a chance."

"Did you get in touch with your boy?"

"Yes, as a matter of fact, he's standing right next to me. Would you like me to send your regards?"

"Is he gonna meet me or not?"

"Oh, he will, he will. He said he wouldn't miss it for anything. He's so excited."

"Where?"

"He said there's an abandoned building off the boulevard, I believe it used to be some type of factory, are you aware of it?"

"I know it."

"Good. What time should I tell him of your arrival?"

"Midnight."

"An excellent choice, you'll get the full moon affect."

"After I'm done with him, I'm coming back for you Marcus."

"If only it were so. Goodbye Ray, it's been a pleasure."

Spencer didn't say anything back, he just hung up.

"What are you doing?" Samantha asked.

"I'm meeting that guy tonight."

"I don't know if that's a good idea."

"This has to end. I can't keep running from both sides."

"But he's a professional. You've never killed anyone."

"First time for everything."

Samantha couldn't hide her concern. She didn't think he could handle the hitman on his own. She figured the best thing she could do is hurry up and get the tape to Collins and maybe they could avoid dealing with the hitman later. Spencer's dad came over to talk to him about the situation.

"Even if you meet that guy tonight, and you do kill him, that's not really gonna change anything. It won't prove that you are innocent."

"But it'll mean one less person that I have to worry about. Right now I'm running from both sides of the law. I have to worry about the police, Marcus' bunch, and making sure you guys are safe. If they're eliminated, I don't have to worry about you guys. All I have to do is avoid the cops."

"I don't really like it."

"I don't either. But it's time I stop being defensive about everything and start being aggressive."

Samantha took a cab to drop off the tape at the FBI building and was back within an hour.

"How'd everything go?" Spencer asked.

"Fine."

"Any problems?"

"No, I said I was in a hurry and if they could just give the tape to Agent Collins, and they said OK."

"I guess I should call there in a little bit to make sure he got it."

Collins and Scott were already in the office talking when Stewart came walking in with the tape.

"Someone dropped this off for you, chief," Stewart said, putting the tape on his desk.

"Where'd you get this?"

"A woman dropped it off a little while ago."

"What'd she look like?"

"They said she was an attractive blonde. Sound familiar?"

"Well let's give it a listen. Pop it in," Collins said, tossing it to Scott.

They listened intently to what was on the tape for several minutes. They replayed it a few more times just to make sure they didn't miss anything.

"Well what do you make of that, gentlemen? Alright, play it again, and let's go over this thing," Collins stated.

They played it again, this time giving commentary to what they were listening to.

"Alright, he comes in, punches him, beats him up for a few minutes," Collins notes.

"Marcus tries to get away but Spencer follows him," Stewart adds.

"He beats him up some more, then pulls a gun," Collins added.

They all fell silent though when Marcus basically admitted that he had Stacey killed. They continued to listen until Spencer asked about a briefcase.

"I knew there was a briefcase!" Collins shouted.

"What do you make of all that?" Scott chimed in.

"Well, Marcus basically admitted that he had the girlfriend killed, there's a hitman after him, Hartwell's crooked, and he's erased evidence. I guess the question is do we believe it," Collins stated.

"Why wouldn't we?" Scott asked him back.

"Cause he had a gun pointed at him. If I'm a regular guy and you point a gun at me, I'll tell you whatever you want to hear. Don't matter to me how bad it makes me look if it lets me see another day."

"I see your point."

"But that don't mean that's what's happened here, either."

"So what are you thinking?" Stewart asked.

"I don't know."

They sat there talking for a few more minutes before deciding to go see Marcus. They figured if they played the tape in front of him, they could read his expressions and mannerisms.

"Let's go talk to the man himself and see what he's got to say," Collins said.

They arrived at Marcus' house a short time later. They knocked on the door for several minutes without getting an answer.

"Maybe he's not home," Stewart guessed.

"His car's here," Collins responded, looking at the driveway.

Stewart continued to knock several more times without a response. Collins directed Scott to take a look around the back. Stewart went over to a window and looked in, but all he saw was an empty room. Scott came back around and reported nothing unusual. Everything seemed to be normal. Collins was getting a feeling though that something was wrong. He wasn't sure what, but something wasn't right. He didn't think Marcus would go anywhere without taking his car. It was his status symbol. Collins was growing increasingly uneasy.

"I'm going in," Collins told them.

"You can't do that," Stewart replied.

"Why not?"

"We don't have a reason or a warrant."

"Well the door's already open."

"No it's not," Stewart said, looking at the door.

"Now it is," Collins said as he kicked the door open.

Stewart tilted his head up, looked at the sky, and shook his head.

"See, the door's already open," Collins told him, pointing at the new opening.

The agents started walking through the house with their guns drawn. They were ready for anything. They each went in separate directions. Scott started searching the living room, Stewart the bedroom, and Collins took the kitchen area. Stewart had made it into the office when he saw a pair of legs coming out from behind the desk. He rushed over and saw Wilson Marcus lying on the floor, blood soaking his shirt and the floor beneath him. He was dead.

"Bill, get in here!" Stewart shouted.

Collins and Scott both rushed in upon hearing Stewart and saw the lifeless body.

"Damn," Collins stated.

"Looks like he was shot through the heart," Stewart noted.

"There's a casing by your foot, Marty," Collins said.

"Spencer had a gun on him. Maybe after he stopped the tape, he pulled the trigger," Stewart analyzed.

"Possible. Or maybe it was that hitman we're hearing about."

"You really putting stock in that?" Stewart asked.

"I think we've got to cover all the possibilities," Collins replied.

Collins told Scott to bring out a team to cover the scene and gather the evidence.

"Even if everything on the tape was true, the other two murders were with a knife. This is a different pattern. This was done by a gun, a gun we know Spencer has," Stewart noted.

"So you're thinking that if it was the hitman he would've killed him with a knife, continuing the pattern," Collins stated.

"Yeah."

"Possible. Unless he was trying to set Spencer up again."

Escape

The agents went outside and started talking about where they thought Spencer was.

"Where would he be right now?" Collins asked.

"Probably at some hotel," Stewart answered.

"What about his parents house?"

"He hasn't shown any interest in contacting them so far. I think he's keeping away from them to keep them out of danger," Stewart said.

"Alright, let's go back to the office to sort this crap out," Collins told the group.

11

Spencer was pacing around the living room wondering what he should do next. Samantha was just watching him pace while his parents were watching TV.

"Should I call to see what they think of the tape?" Spencer asked everyone.

"Probably. I'm sure they've listened to it several times by now," Samantha answered.

"I guess I'll be back in a little bit then," Spencer said.

"Where are you going?" Samantha asked.

"I don't want to call from here in case they trace the call."

"I guess that makes sense. I'll come with you."

"No, you stay here. I won't be very long."

Spencer put on a baseball hat and sunglasses and ducked out the back hopping over the fence and cutting through neighboring houses yards. He was careful to not stay out in open spaces too long. He walked near bushes and trees, close to buildings and cars, anyplace that he could quickly hide behind should he have to at a moments notice. He walked for about ten minutes when he came across a pay phone at a convenience store. He called the FBI building and asked to speak with Agent Collins on an urgent matter. It seemed like he was waiting for an eternity, but within 30 seconds Collins picked up the phone.

"Collins here."

"Did you get the tape?" Spencer asked.

"Who is this?"

"Ray Spencer."

"At last we finally have the chance to talk."

"Did you get it?"

"Yes."

"What'd you think of it?"

"It was very interesting."

"That proves that I'm innocent of everything, right?" Spencer wondered.

Collins hesitated briefly before answering.

"Not quite."

"Why not? You heard everything. Marcus admitted there's a cover-up, that he had Stacey killed, that someone's after me, what more do you want?"

"First, you had a gun pointed at him."

"That's the only way I could get him to talk."

"But how do I know it's the truth. Most people will say whatever someone wants them to say when there's a gun pointed at them."

"So how do I convince you?"

"Meet me somewhere."

"No way. You'll arrest me the moment you put your eyes on me."

There was silence between the two men for a few seconds. Spencer didn't know what else to say. He resigned himself to the situation.

"Well, thanks for the time," Spencer said, about to hang up the phone.

"Wait, don't hang up," Collins pleaded.

"Why, so you can trace me? You don't believe me, I'm not waiting for a cop car to pull up any minute."

"I give you my word we're not tracing the call."

"Why should I believe that?"

"Cause I'm asking you to. I'm giving you my word. You want me to believe you're innocent. Make me believe it."

"How do I do that?"

"Just talk to me. Tell me your side of things."

"Where do you want me to start?"

"If you're innocent, why didn't you come to us in the beginning?"

"I was told that if I did, my family would be killed. I couldn't take that chance."

"I can understand that," Collins told him, trying to calm Spencer's reservations. "How'd you leave Marcus' house?"

"What do you mean?"

"Was he alive, dead, hurt, what?"

"He was sitting in his chair. He had a few cuts on his face. Why does it matter?"

"Cause Wilson Marcus is dead."

"He can't be. I just talked to him earlier."

"He's dead, Ray. Shot through the chest. You had a gun on him. You see why I have doubts?"

"I didn't kill him."

"How do I know?"

"Cause I give you my word. Mine's as good as yours."

"Who else would kill him?"

"Probably the hitman that's following me. He was there with Marcus when I talked to him earlier. He's doing the same thing he did with Stacey and Hurst, making it look like I did it. If he can't find me to kill me, he'll frame me to make sure I go to jail."

"So do you have any type of evidence to prove anything you say?"

"No," Spencer said with a sigh.

"Where's Samantha fit into all of this? You know we could arrest her as an accomplice."

"She's completely innocent. She's never done anything. I forced her to take me places at gunpoint."

"I don't think I quite believe that."

"Please just leave her be."

"I'm not really interested in her, Ray. I'm interested in you. I want to believe your story, I really do. But I also need to find you soon. Since this thing started bodies are piling up. I don't want anymore."

"It'll all be over after tonight."

"Why tonight?"

Spencer hesitated on telling him.

"Talk to me, Ray," Collins insisted.

"Just trust me. No more bodies after tonight."

"So there'll be one more?"

"That's all I can say. I really have to go."

"What's the hurry?"

"I'm getting nervous. I have to go."

Collins tried to get him to keep talking but all he heard was a buzzing sound that accompanied the hung up phone. Collins summoned for Stewart and Scott to come into his office.

"I just got a phone call from Ray Spencer," Collins told his fellow agents, who were a little stunned and surprised.

"What'd he say?" Stewart asked.

"Told me he was innocent."

"What about Marcus?"

"He said he didn't do it."

"What do you think, chief?"

Collins thought for a few seconds before carefully choosing his words.

"Well...you know from the very beginning I've been cautious about this case. I've never been sold on Spencer being guilty. I really...think...he's innocent. Especially after talking to him, I believe him. I do."

"So what's the next move?" Scott asked.

"We have to find him," Collins answered.

"Did he say anything that would indicate where he was?" Stewart asked.

"No, but we need to find him tonight. He said everything ends tonight. One more body before it's over."

"One more? What do you make of that?" Stewart wondered.

"I'd say that would be the hitman…or Spencer."

"So they've set something up," Stewart realized.

"We gotta find him," Collins said.

"But where?" Scott asked.

"Everywhere," Collins replied.

They got a few teams together and took to the streets. They figured the meeting would happen in a more private area, so they patrolled the areas where less people frequented.

Once Spencer returned to the house everyone could tell something was wrong.

"What's the matter?" Samantha asked.

"Marcus is dead."

"What? How?"

"I don't know. He was shot. The hitman must have shot him right after we hung up. Trying to frame another one on me I guess."

"Did you talk to Collins?" she asked.

"Yeah."

"And?"

"He still has doubts."

"So what now?"

"Same as before. It all ends tonight."

As soon as Samantha heard him say that she put her head down. She didn't think he had much of a chance against a professional killer. A couple hours wound up passing without much conversation. Everyone seemed to know what the likely outcome was going to be. They were glad there'd finally be a conclusion but it wasn't the one they were hoping for. As the time approached for Spencer to leave he didn't really want to say goodbye to anyone. He wanted them to think positively that he would return. He shook his father's hand before hugging him, and then hugged his crying mother. He then walked over to Samantha and gave her a hug before kissing her on the cheek.

"I can never thank you enough," he told her.

"You can thank me by coming back."

He shook his head in agreement. Spencer grabbed his gun off a table and tucked it into his belt letting his shirt cover it. Before walking out the door he looked back at them fully aware that it could be the last time he ever saw them again. He had butterflies flying around in his stomach, nervous about what was about to happen. But at the same time he was glad it was coming to a finish. He got into the cab waiting for him. He felt anxious during the ride as he thought about meeting his opponent. As he approached the abandoned warehouse the butterflies had gotten ten times worse than before. His heart was pounding so hard he thought he was having a heart attack.

Closing in on the warehouse Spencer didn't see a car but he could sense someone else was already there. He stepped out of the cab and immediately sprinted over to the building. He put his one hand on the handle of the door while removing the gun out of his belt with the other. He looked up to the sky, his hand beginning to sweat, and taking a deep sigh.

Spencer swung the door open quickly and dove into the building hitting the concrete floor ready to fire. He turned his head in every direction without seeing a thing in sight. He squinted his eyes but it was so dark, he could hardly see his own hand. He backed up against the wall and slowly slid his way down the wall to his right. As he was moving a loud piercing shot rang out just missing the side of his face blistering the wall behind him. Spencer dropped to the floor taking cover behind a large wooden crate.

"Why don't you come out so we can settle this man to man," Spencer yelled out.

"I'm fine right here," a voice yelled back.

Spencer peered over the crate trying to make out some type of human form in the distance without much luck. He flipped the lid of the crate up slightly letting it hit and crackle back down to create a noise that he hoped would draw fire. It worked. Just as the lid hit back down he noticed a flash from the gunfire in the back of the warehouse. Spencer crawled around the crate to a series of stacked boxes. He looked around to see if he could make anything out. He thought he could see a couple crates toward the direction of the gunfire. He let a shot rip into one of the crates in that direction. He heard some movement.

"We could spend hours doing this. It's not gonna get us anywhere," Spencer shouted.

"So what do you suggest?" the voice replied.

"Let's meet in the middle."

"What do you want…gunfight at the OK Corral?"

"Why not?"

"I don't think I trust you."

Silence embraced the building for a few minutes as both men were figuring out their next move. Spencer crawled from the boxes to the wall. He kept crawling against the wall till he came across another door. It looked like it used to be an office. Spencer grabbed hold of the bottom of the door and slammed it shut.

The hitman saw the door open and close and thinking that Spencer went inside started to run towards it. As soon as he got to the door Spencer saw his outline and sprung up to shoot. The hitman saw him out of the corner of his eye and turned towards him. They fired simultaneously. Both men went down, their guns flying from their hands. They both got to their knees and stumbled to their feet.

Spencer was bent over holding his left hip, which was bleeding. He looked over and saw his opponent in pain, but looked like he was recovering, and started searching for his gun. The hitman stumbled back into the wall, taking his mask off, breathing heavily. He'd been shot in the chest near his heart. He noticed his gun lying on the floor and fell down to get it. He gripped it in his hand and turned towards Spencer who was still trying to find his weapon. He fired and shot Spencer again, causing Spencer to fall backwards.

Spencer was lying on his back, pain shooting from his hip along with the new hole in his right shoulder. He looked up and saw his attacker standing over him. He closed his eyes waiting for it to be over. A shot rang out in the darkness. Spencer felt the man falling into him. Spencer pushed the lifeless body to the side of him. He slowly got to his feet and saw a group of people running towards him.

"Ray Spencer I presume?" one man asked him.

"Who are you?" he wearily replied.

"I'm Agent Collins."

"How'd you know who you were shooting?"

"Who said we knew?" Collins said with a smirk.

"Forgive me if I don't shake your hand," Spencer sarcastically said, bending over in tremendous pain from his hip.

"Just hang on; the ambulance should be here in a few minutes."

"Easy for you to say," he said before falling over and passing out.

Spencer woke up in the hospital the next day. He looked over and saw Samantha sitting there beside him.

"Hey, look who's awake," she said smiling.

"What's going on?"

"Well, you underwent surgery. They took the bullets out of your hip and shoulder," she informed him.

"So what's the verdict?"

"You're gonna be fine," she said while stroking his hair.

"What about everything else?"

"I don't know."

They talked for a few more minutes before the door opened for another visitor. It was Collins.

"So how're you feeling?" Collins said enthusiastically.

"Like I just been shot."

"I like a sense of humor. Anything I can get ya?"

"A new life?"

"Done."

"Huh?"

"You want a new life, you got it," he said looking around the room, smiling.

"What, a new life in prison?"

"Nope. A new life out there," Collins told him, pointing out the window.

"How's that?" Spencer wondered.

"You've been cleared. You're free to go on your way as soon as you're well enough to leave here."

"Are you serious?"

"Do I look like I kid around?"

"Actually, yeah."

"Well, yeah, I do. But not in this case. We found the hitman's car parked outside that warehouse, along with your briefcase, and some other incriminating paperwork. All of which clears you in the process."

Spencer just looked over to Samantha, not quite believing what he was hearing.

"How'd you guys find us there anyway?" Spencer asked.

"We got an anonymous phone call," Collins replied, looking over to Samantha.

Spencer looked to Samantha, who put her eyes towards the floor, not sure if he'd be unhappy with her.

"Lucky she did. You'd have been dead if she hadn't," Collins told him.

"I can never thank her enough," Spencer said, grabbing Saman-tha's hand to hold.

"So what do you plan to do next, go back to accounting?" Collins wondered.

"I don't know. It's a more dangerous field than I thought."

"Well, if you choose something different, we're always hiring," he said with a smile.

Collins shook hands with Spencer before going on his way and wished him luck.

"What do you plan on doing when you get out of here?" Samantha wondered.

"I'm not sure, but I know I'll need a new place to live. I'll never be able to live in my house again."

"I know of a place you could go," she hinted.

"Are you offering me a place to stay?"

"If you're interested," She replied

"I was hoping you'd ask," he admitted. "By the way how do you feel about dogs?"

"I love dogs," she said as she leaned over the bed kissing him softly on the lips.

"There's more where that came from," she teased.

"I could get used to this."

About The Author

Rye James was born in Philadelphia, Pa., where he still resides with his wife, daughter, and three dogs. In his spare time he likes to ride horses, spend time with his family, and watch Philly sports teams. Visit him on the web at www.ryejames.bravehost.com where he updates fans on the progress of his future works. He is currently working on several novels and short stories in a variety of genres.

Other Titles Available:

The Assassin (Western)
Day Of The Assassin (Western short story)
Misconduct (Hockey short story)